She narrowed her gaze, and whispered. "You're a starin' at me like ya' did when you kissed me, Gambler. You about to do that again?"

He found her abrupt. "Would you want me to?"

She sipped lemonade and set the glass back on the crate. "I liked it all right, but it made my lips tingle and..." She went on, her cheeks flushing pink. "Did you like it...when you did it to me, cause I ain't ever been kissed a 'fore you?"

"I liked it very much." He leaned in taking a small kiss across her tender lips and then nipped a second. "You smell like that lilac perfume Laurel brought to you."

"You want me to open up my mouth, Gambler?" She left her lips partially open.

Well, she could change the mood real fast. He held up a finger and smiled anyway. "Not supposed to ask. Let me show you what I mean. Lay back."

"You ain't gonna try to poke me are you, Gambler?" Her mouth dropped open.

He fell to his back beside her, defeated. This woman was gonna take a lot of fine tuning.

Deuces Wyld

by

Kim Turner

The Wylder West

Deuces Wyld

Cover Art by *Debbie Taylor*

The Wild Rose Press, Inc.
PO Box 708
Adams Basin, NY 14410-0708
Visit us at www.thewildrosepress.com

Publishing History
First Edition, 2022
Trade Paperback ISBN 978-1-5092-4169-9
Digital ISBN 978-1-5092-4170-5

The Wylder West
Published in the United States of America

Dedication

For Mom...because it was never easy raising a tomboy daughter, and for Dad who taught me at a young age not to gamble.

~

To my husband, Chuck, who still picks up all the pieces so I have time to write with the crazy of our daily lives.

~

And for Dennie Garrett and Nicki Reed...girls, its time for another road trip to see the boys in the band!

Acknowledgments

Thanks to Dawson McBride for narrating my cowboys exactly as I imagine them to be. There is nothing like listening to one of my stories coming to life, and I cannot wait to hear your voice as Dalton Payne in this one.

And to my Dad, David (NY NICK) Nicolich, and Michelle Chambers, I appreciate all the help with the game of poker and how it was played back in the day. I thank you all from the bottom of my heart!

Chapter One

Wylder, Wyoming Territory, Fall 1878

Dalton Payne glanced out the dust-covered window across the high plains of southern Wyoming, his father's voice playing through his head.

Forgiveness comes and time heals all things, son.

Traveling back home and the long train ride down memory lane brought it all back with the news of his father's passing. He should've returned long before now, but penance was paid one day at a time, sucking the soul right out of a man's chest.

Most passengers were still sleeping as daybreak began to brighten the railroad car. He glimpsed at the young man sitting alone on the front bench, the same lad who hadn't eaten a thing for the leg of the journey. The kid of maybe twelve had lifted the change purse of the woman seated behind him.

Dalton stood, taking up the cane he used most all the time, stretching his bad leg and his back. If he played his cards right and added a bit of charm to the situation, he'd manage to set things right for the boy who was no doubt headed for more trouble.

He stepped closer to the front of the car and sat by the boy, who eyed him with suspicion as he rested a hand on his cane. "Wylder's ahead, you gettin' off there?"

The youth nodded but said nothing, his hands folded before him, his clothing much too small and worn beyond wear.

He chose his words with care and softened his voice. "About fifteen more miles of track left to make things right."

The boy gave him a sharp glance. "Don't know what you're talking about, mister."

"Oh, I think you do." He pointed the tip of his cane toward the kid's coat pocket and lifted the small purse of coins. "Now, I'm suggesting while everyone's still quiet that you slip this back where it came from and no one has to know, 'cept you and me."

Angry blue eyes held his gaze in a stand-off.

"I've read a lot of faces, kid. I've seen all the tricks there are." He took a deep breath, trying to sound convincing. "You've the choice. Make it a good one."

The lad glared, snatching the pouch and with caution set it back into the bag of the woman who still slept behind them. He faced the front once more but kept his eyes down, caught red-handed. At least he was smart enough to figure out the right thing to do.

He rested both hands on the head of the cane as the train rambled through a rough section of track. "Best when you step down to Wylder, you find a different line of work. What's your name, kid?"

The boy folded his arms and gave a reluctant shrug. "Gideon."

"Gideon, find some real work when you get to Wylder. Thieving isn't very lucrative for any length of time." He stood and handed the kid ten dollars in paper money and a wrapped biscuit with bacon inside.

With a bit of hesitation, Gideon shoved the money

into his pocket and unwrapped the biscuit. "How'd you know, thought you were sleepin'?"

"Gambler's sleep with one eye open, kid." He gave a wink.

With that he went back to his seat. He'd watched during the night as the boy had taken the coins, but the kid wouldn't have a chance in a western town as a thief. He'd wind up on the wrong end of a gun. He'd seen the like in the big cities and the small towns and he'd read the kid's face. He was hungry, alone and afraid, but he was no thief.

And was he any different than the boy, lost along some forgotten track of trying to find his way home. He'd spent a good deal of time on the train thinking and his conclusion was that he was tired. So damn tired of it all, of drifting from town to town to call no place home. Tired of the game that had filled his pockets with more money than he'd spend in a lifetime. So, he was going to pay his respects to his father and settle down on the homestead left behind. Work the land, live a quiet life, rest his knee. And maybe find peace of some semblance.

Too bad his father wouldn't be there to see him step off the train dressed in as fine a suit as any city slicker from back East. His name was well-known and he'd never have to work again, unless he wanted to.

"Town of Wylder folks. We'll be stopping an hour before we pull out again." The car conductor slapped a blue uniform hat back on his head and bent to glance out the window. The screeching of train brakes tossed steam and dust into the air as the locomotive began to slow, arriving at the Wylder depot.

Dalton waited for the immediate scramble of

patrons to leave the train, the kid eyeing him once more as he stepped from the car. He tugged the watch from his vest pocket and leaned on his cane to stand. A bit before seven and Wylder was already coming to life, the depot busy and town bustling with activity. He picked up his satchel and tossed the saddle bags over his shoulder as he stepped down to the earth and inhaled a deep breath of confidence, scanning across town. While there was nothing to prove to anyone, it wasn't often a town forgot the past.

"Welcome home, Mr. Payne." The conductor tipped his hat. "You can collect your horse at the last car, sir." He was used to the treatment, those who respected him and the game, his name preceding him. But for the most part that came with money. People respected money and Wylder would be no different when it came down to it.

"He tipped the man a coin as he walked toward the last car, where Sable was being unloaded, the horse anxious in the hands of two men from the railroad.

"Thank you. I've got her. Easy girl." He took the reins and Sable calmed with a last snort of annoyance.

One of the men nodded toward the Black Bay. "She's sure a beauty, Mr. Payne."

"That she is." He tipped both as he laid his bags over the already saddled horse.

"You gotta poker set here in town, Mr. Payne?" The younger of the two asked, his eyes wide with wonder.

"No, Boys I'm retired as of right now. Home to stay." He led Sable ahead, making his way toward the land office to claim the deed for his father's homestead. Wylder had grown, the town far busier than he remembered. More buildings, more people and everyone in a hurry. Shop keepers held in doorways, wagons and men on horseback filled the streets as women browsed the markets.

As he passed the Five Star Saloon, he touched the revolver riding in the holster buckled low around his hips. Wasn't many a gambling man that didn't own some way of protecting their interests in lawless western towns.

He tied Sable outside the land office and in less than ten minutes returned to the horse, the deed inside the pocket of his black duster, along with the list of supplies he'd need to purchase at the mercantile. He headed that way, taking in the town he'd left fifteen years ago, for reasons he still wasn't sure he understood. One card game too many, the greed of men and a woman who'd taken out his knee and left him no choice but to leave town. Well, he was returning home for good and held his head high. He owed no one in the town of Wylder a thing.

****

It was nearing noon by the time Dalton topped the ridge. He studied his father's overgrown homestead. Sable rocked her head as he stopped her. The ride from town wasn't long, only a few miles, but he'd taken his time. Strange he'd never seen the place he'd purchased in cash for his father with the winnings out of a big pot in San Francisco years back.

He scanned the property and urged Sable down the slope, spotting the wooden cross in the field behind the house. He sucked in a deep breath, the pain of losing his father visceral as it scored through the center of his heart. His father had been a good man, the best father anyone could ever have. He'd raised Dalton alone and always done right by him, even taking a switch to him when it was needed. More times than not he'd deserved it. He smiled at the thought, in spite of the loss that threatened tears.

Sable sniffed the air as they approached the house. The horse knew home as well as he did, the clean breath of a fresh meadow of green and the promise of—home. The whitewashed clapboard home with a big front porch had seen better days and could use a little paint and fixing up. And the yard was in need of a good clean up, nothing hard work wouldn't fix.

He dismounted and tied the horse, eyeing the barn, which needed repairs to the roof. He studied his palms. The smooth hands of a man of cards but it wouldn't take much hard work to rough them up.

His mind made up, he nodded. First things first though. He made his way behind the house, toward his father's grave, the dirt little settled before the wooden cross.

'*Hiram Payne. 1800-1878*'.

Seventy-eight years and this was all that marked a man's life. A good life. Bending to a knee, he rested his hand on the exposed earth, propping his cane across his good leg.

"I'm sorry, Papa." Never much of a praying man, he bowed his head in respect and uttered silent words. He stood and turned back toward the cabin, walking to the front and taking the steps to the porch. As he touched the front door, it fell from its hinges. "A new door then." He leaned it against the wall and stepped inside.

Streaks of sunlight filtered in through the dust

covered windows and cobwebs strung from the ceiling, heavier in the corners of the room.

The house still held his father's things, a coat over one of the chairs at the small wooden table, a cane propped near the door and his father's brown hat on the hook by the door. He touched the coat as he moved to check each of the other rooms, lingering at the one with his father's bed, the quilt familiar, made by his mother long before his birth.

On the night table the picture of his parents from their wedding day, a year before his birth and the loss of the mother he'd never known had always hurt as if something he couldn't touch was missing. He lifted the frame. His father, a young man with a bright smile and his mother's eyes very much like his own. They should have been buried together but his mother lay somewhere in Nebraska that he couldn't remember.

He turned around, noting the other smaller picture by his father's bed. Him as a youth with a smile like a bandit and ready to shoot down hell. Well, besides a couple of major mishaps, he'd done that, taken on the biggest names in poker, leaving his mark on the world. And so was the price to fame and fortune, other losses that could never be regained.

He stepped into the next room that held two small beds, still made up. Previous owners must have had children and his father had left things as they had been. He moved back to the main room and made a mental list of purchases for his next trip into town. With another single look around, he limped back outside to Sable and grabbed the sack of food staples he'd purchased earlier.

"Well, Sable, I do believe we're home, girl." He

gave the horse a soft pat and made his way back inside.

Chapter Two

Leona Fabray set aside the heavy wooden paddle she used to stir the clothing soaking in the pot, and brushed a forearm across her sweaty brow.

"Whew, already a hot 'un this mornin'." She'd started the small fires for laundry earlier, but noted even for late September the heat of a Wyoming summer had little relented. "And as soon as I get ta' sewing like Laurel's a teachin' me, I ain't a gonna wash another sappin' thang in heat like this."

"You might get to that sooner than you think since Laurel is teaching you to sew." Mary McCleary moved a hot iron across a pair of trousers, giving her a nod from inside the dress shop.

"She says I'm a doin' right fine." She continued her work. Laurel Holt had been teaching her the skills it took to mend and sew new clothing. And one day she was gonna walk right up to the Widow Lowery and tell her she'd be a sewin' and no longer washing. Yep, that's what she was gonna do. No more a washin' dirty drawers for the no goods rolling through town all the time.

She lifted the floppy brown hat to tuck her long, dark hair up into it. Sweat rolled down her neck and back, dampening the oversize linen shirt that hung over brown pants that were several sizes too big.

Widow Lowery stepped outside and set a heaping

basket of clothing on the table. "Took in more wash, Miss Fabray. You'll need all this done today and with this heat it'll surely have time to dry before the afternoon."

The elderly, rotund woman ran a lace lined handkerchief across her brow.

"Got two pot's a goin'." Leona grumbled as she scrubbed a miner's shirt across a metal washboard and dropped it back into the dingy gray water.

"Add the third one, it's going to be a busy day." The widow turned in a huff to head back inside the dress shop.

"Yes'm, Widow Lowery." She mocked her employer with a frown and eyed the third bucket she'd yet to fire up. It still held the cold soapy used water from yesterday. "Light the third pot. Ain't her that's gotta stand out here stirrin' these pots from hell's fires if'n I know anything 'bout it."

Mary lifted her brows and went back to her work with the iron.

It wasn't that she minded the widow bossin' her all the time, but of late each day brought more to do. She supposed when it came down to it, talkin' to herself made the workday go faster. Besides she needed the job if she was plannin' on eatin' and feeding Ernest, the mule she'd managed to purchase a month back. The ornery cuss was all she'd been able to afford from the livery, but he made the ride out to see Laurel, and her son Jesse, easier.

Just as she tilted the pot a pair of black boots appeared. Gray water sloshed over the top of the shiny leather, ankle high, before she could stop it.

She lifted her gaze up the length of the fancy black

trousers, low riding brown leather holster holding a shiny revolver, up to the gray vest and then to the greenest eyes of a stranger she'd ever seen. He stood taller than most, with a trimmed beard and shoulder length dark hair. He held a cane in his right hand, which he lifted from the wash water.

She gulped, expecting a good scolding. "Mister, better watch where you're a steppin' in these parts."

He peered down at his boots, though she didn't give him a chance to say anything more. He had a bag of clothing in one hand and a cane in the other.

"Doin' my job and you should know ain't no business for yer bag of clothes on the side of the dress shop. Hand 'em over." She reached for the bag he held and plopped it on the table behind her, still expecting a good tongue lashing that never came. "I reckon I can get yours all washed up since I done wet your boots."

The sight of the stick he leaned on, made her feel worse about things, but he wasn't an old man, maybe nearing his forties if she were guessing right. It didn't go past her he was right handsome as he lifted his green eyes to her once more.

A smile crossed his face in spite of the situation as if he was amused. "Seems the last time I was in Wylder the door was on this side."

"Mister, you ain't been around here in a long time if'n you remember that." She studied him; certain she'd never seen his likes before. She focused back on her work; a bit overwhelmed by his continued stare.

"I was from here once, long time ago. Dalton Payne." He introduced himself, holding out a hand, which she ignored since her own hands were wet and soapy.

"Well, sit on down an' take those boots off to dry and I'll get yer socks all washed." She steered him toward the porch, though it was hard to take her eyes from him. His fancy black suit was as nifty as she'd ever seen, and he walked with an air of confidence. But more than that he never took his gaze from her. "Least I can do."

He sat, leaning his cane aside and began with his boots, still eyeing her from under that dark hat. "Do I have the pleasure of learning who it is that will be drying my boots and washing my clothing then?"

Why did heat cross her cheeks when he held those green eyes on her? She turned back to her work shoving logs under the empty pot. "I'm Leona Fabray if'n it's any business of yourn."

She reached out to take his socks, but instead he gripped her hand, turning her to face him. "Nice to meet you, Ms. Fabray. But I'll make you a deal. Is that your mule there?" He let go and pointed a thumb over his shoulder toward Ernest.

"Yep." She gave him a speculative glance as she rung his socks. "He's mine all right, an ornery cuss at times."

"I'd like to borrow him for an afternoon, help me plow a small garden for starters, and I'll still pay you for the wash and for his use." He gave her a big smile, though the idea made her a bit uncertain as he went on. "Got a bad knee, need a bit of help as I'm taking over the Payne homestead, my father's old place."

She looked back at Ernest. The Payne homestead wasn't too far outside of town. She'd heard old Mr. Payne had passed a month or more back. "Mister, ain't many used to loaning out a mule without it gettin' stolen around these parts. How do I know I can trust you from any other dirt dobber that runs through here?"

"I've no reason to harm him or keep him. Just need to plow a small garden. I've got a horse there, but she's not meant to be behind a plow and seein' you have my clothing, I wouldn't get far." He pointed to a solid black mare tied at the post.

She tossed his socks into the first boiling pot. She bent to pick up a piece of already flaming wood from under it and added it to wood under the waiting kettle fanning it to ignite. "I reckon you can borrow him then. But I'll remind you horse thieving will get ya' hanged here in Wylder. And you're gonna be a payin' me for his use?"

He nodded, still wearing that silly smile. Well, most men didn't take to her, so he was either funnin' her or serious about the use of the mule.

She reached for the two buckets of water to fill the third pot, but he beat her to it, limping as he poured one bucket after another for her.

"Mr. Payne, this here's *my* job. You'll have to go and find yer own." She dusted her hands and lifted his socks to scrub each across the board in the bucket of sudsy gray water.

"Just helping you out." He sat again dusting the sand from his bare feet. "Gotta sit here for a bit, might as well be useful while I'm at it."

Two men turned the corner, both walking along the sand covered street. One spoke to the other, slapping him on the back. "Hey it's him, Slim. Sure 'nough like you said."

"You're the famous Dalton Payne." The second man trotted right up to him and grabbed his hand, shaking it until Dalton pulled it away and wiped it along his dark trousers. "Biggest poker champion there is and back in Wylder to boot."

Leona stepped back when Mr. Payne settled a hand to the gun at his hip. She'd lived in Wylder long enough to know where respect was due.

"You here for a game or off to another?" The first man asked, a toothless grin spreading across his bearded face.

Dalton eased a hand away from the revolver, with a nod.

Leona wrung out the socks, twisting tight to rid them of excess water. They were fancier then she'd washed in a while, making her wonder if he was as famous a gambler as they suggested. She suspected it was true given how fine a black suit he wore. Not many in Wylder wore the same 'ceptin for the bankers and those with money.

"Sorry, boys, I'm retired." He smiled, showing dimples not hidden by his trimmed beard. Why couldn't she stop a lookin' at him?

"Ain't a gambler ever alive given it up for good, we all know that." The second man nudged his counterpart in the side. "The game'll find you if ya' don't find it."

He tipped his hat. "You two men have yourself a nice day."

Both men snickered, back slapping each other as they moseyed off still talking about Dalton Payne, winningest gambler ever at the tables.

"Famous gambler? Guess that explains the fine clothing you're a wearin' then." She folded her arms, waiting for his next response.

He inspected himself. "Just a gentleman's dress."

City slickers came through town all the time, most looking to make more money at swindling or cheating others if she knew anything about it. "Reckon not. Here's yer socks and you'll just have to walk around a bit soggy today in those fancy boots. Leave 'em outside over- night and they'll be like new 'uns by morning. Though you'd best check 'em for critters 'afore you put your feet in 'em."

He focused on her, taking the damp stockings. "I do thank you, Mrs. Fabray, for the advice and the wash."

"Oh, I ain't married. Just Miss, but call me Leona, like all the rest." She corrected him. "I'll have your clothes done by the late afternoon so you can get back to gambling or the like."

He gave a hearty laugh. "Like I said I'm retired, looking forward to working the homestead. A dream a long time comin'."

"Dreamin' of a homestead?" She asked as she stirred the new pot. "Ain't much dreamin' in that but a lot of hard work if'n I know of it, but I wouldn't likely mind that myself."

"Just looking to work the land, fix up the place is all. What about you?" He angled his head to hold her in his sights still.

"What about me?" She leaned the paddle aside and folded her arms, lifting her full attention to him. He sure was a bit nosey now wasn't he?

"You got any dreams, something you wanna do or see one day?" He asked as he tugged his socks on and stepped into each boot, rubbing his right knee, taking up the cane.

"Maybe." She had dreams, but she sure wasn't use to anyone much caring about her ideas. "I's thinkin' one day I might like to see the ocean. Read a lot of books about it." She narrowed her focus. "But if'n I like to eat, I gotta keep this here job and you're a slowin' me down, Gambler. And watch where your steppin' next time. Lucky for you wasn't no hot water I was a pourin' out."

"Will heed your advice." He stood and tipped his black hat. "Miss Leona, may you one day see the mighty Pacific in all its glory of blue. It's indeed a fine thing. I'll pick up the rest of my wash later in the week and see about the mule."

She couldn't help a smile as she went back to her work and he made off to the black mare, she also couldn't help herself in looking on as he headed the horse outside of town.

"I think that gambler had eyes for you." Mary moved her iron across the hard board before her, still working inside the door.

Leona scanned the direction Mr. Payne had ridden off, but he had disappeared. "Nahh, he just wants to borrow Ernest, if'n I know anything about it."

****

Dalton added the merchandise he'd purchased at the mercantile to the saddle bags across Sable. He'd bought several sets of work clothing and a pair of boots for homestead chores which he planned to start soon enough. He tugged the horse behind him and as he moved through town, peered at the Lowery Dress Shoppe. Leona was outside at her pots, scrubbing hard at her work. He watched her as he went by, wondering why she appeared as she did in oversized clothing that might have had its better day. He suspected underneath that sloppy pile of clothing and floppy hat was a woman who'd remained hidden from the likes of men in Wylder, given those amber eyes and dark hair. She was beautiful though he suspected she had never realized that about herself, given her appearance.

He let his gaze drift past her, turned toward the saloon and took a deep breath. What was a young unmarried woman doing all alone in a town like Wylder? He had no business questioning anything about her, except she'd crossed his mind over and over since the morning she'd poured water across his boots. Well, those thoughts were best left alone. He hadn't returned home for anything other than peace, quiet and hard work.

Finn Wylder, from the mercantile, had let him know Sonny Cash, who owned the Five Star Saloon, needed to speak with him. The grin on the store owner's face had enlightened his suspicions. The town of Wylder wouldn't be any different than all the rest for the last fifteen years, in wanting his name for a big game. And some things never changed.

He sized up the saloon, a few men loitered at an outside table, none of whom he recognized and one holding a scantily clad red-head on his lap. The woman eyed him as he stepped to the double swinging doors, but he went on inside. Standing inside the doors, he let his eyes adjust to the lesser light. Several tables of men played cards to one side and others sat alone or stood at the bar, but every man turned their stare on him and the large room went silent.

He gave a nod to no one in particular, and made his way to the bar, the tap of his spurs on the hardwood planked floor accented by the knock of his cane.

Heard you were in town, Payne." Sonny Cash held out a hand and a wide smile crossed his face. "Welcome home."

He accepted the outstretched hand. He'd known the man years ago when it all had happened, but it seemed no one so far was calling him out on a past that had dealt him a bad set of cards.

He held the man's gaze as whispers came from the poker playing tables. "Finn Wylder said you had a proposition for me. I'll bet I can guess all about that."

"We'll sit. Can I get you something? On the house of course... no charge." Sonny nodded, though bobbled across his words a bit.

"Sarsaparilla." He'd given up the drink long ago. Some drank while they put their hands to the cards, but he'd never been very good at both. Instead he carried a small flask of bourbon in his coat pocket as a reminder of how alcohol could change things.

The bar owner poured a glass of the dark liquid and grabbed the mug to lead the way to a table. "Sarsaparilla. Still not a drinking man, after all these years."

He wasn't sure if the man was making light of him or remembered well enough how things had happened. Seemed the town was talking his name and more than a few knew he was back and those and others would remember how things went down. Funny he'd thought maybe he wouldn't find much of a welcome in returning to Wylder, but then as his father had told him, *time healed all things*...

"You remember Russ Holt and this here's Doc Coyote Sullivan, best physician all around the territory." Sonny pulled out a chair as Dalton took the doctor's hand and followed to grab Holt's grip, remembering the rancher well.

"Wylder's prodigal son returns." Russ broke into a wide grin, the old man's gray mustache moving as he spoke. "Good to see ya' Dalton."

"Still ranching these parts?" He propped his cane against the table, then sipped from the glass mug, letting the cool liquid quench his parched tongue.

The old rancher tilted his hat back with a nod. "Sorry about your father, Dalton, he's a right good man."

He nodded, not sure he had words, the death of his father still raw at times.

"Look Dalton, we'd.... the town of Wylder, with you here...we want your agreement to set up a poker championship. And with your name, Wylder might bring in the best players, earn some real money for the town." Sonny propped closer, eyes wide, his voice speeding along.

He said nothing as the man went on.

"What'ya say? Of course, you can think on it." The bartender didn't let up, easing back in his chair, fidgeting as if he was nervous.

"I've retired from the game, Gentleman." He sipped again. He'd come to Wylder to leave the cards behind once and for all. "Been a long time coming."

"You can't retire from poker...you wrote the win on the biggest games in all the territories." Sonny's voice climbed an octave as he waved his hands to explain.

The red-head from outside sauntered over and eased right into Dalton's lap. She snuggled up close, her breath against his ear. "Some are sayin' you know cards better than you know a woman. As a woman, I say different."

He studied her lying blue eyes and eased her from his lap, at the same time retrieving the wallet she'd slipped from inside his duster pocket. "Won't be needin' your services Ma'am but you have yourself a nice afternoon." He shoved the wallet back into the pocket of his coat as the woman made off out the swinging doors with a hiss.

"I'm warning you Clementine, you keep that up and I ain't gonna pay you to be here and take care of the tables." Sonny shouted.

Russ chuckled and the doctor lifted his brows.

"Mr. Payne, I took care of your father. Thought you might like to know he didn't suffer. Things were really peaceful," the physician explained, taking up the conversation.

"Thank you, Doctor. He was uhm.... a better man than most." He to keep his emotions intact, the pain of his father's death tangible at times.

"He was very kind...worried more about my visits than his own care. Talked a lot about how proud he was of you and your travels." The doctor was built sturdy, tall and muscular with a gun belt of his own, which wasn't much of a surprise in these parts.

What others thought of his father eased his own conscious little. He'd been successful enough for respect wherever he went, but he'd missed his father. Maybe he'd missed too much for a long damn time.

"Well, Dalton, about the game? Your name could bring people from all over, as far as San Francisco even." Sonny didn't let up on pushing for his participation, though his agitation showed through as he gripped the table edges.

He gave a chuckle, shaking his head. "You worried about the well-being of Wylder's finances or what you'd make with a big game here? I'm retired." He stood, double checking his wallet and taking hold of his cane. "It's good to see you Russ. How's Caleb, still whispering to the horses?" Caleb Holt, Russ' nephew rode like the wind and knew horses better than most.

"Yeah, he's still got the touch, might like to take a look at that mare you have out there." The old cowboy added. "He went and got himself married, got a boy about three years old and his wife's expecting again. We uh…we lost Richard several years back."

"Sorry to hear that. I'll have to stop by to speak to Caleb some time." He offered, though he had no intention of playing poker for any championship.

"You do that." Russ added, sipping the beer before him and set it aside. "That cane come from the last game you played here in Wylder?"

He held the man's stare, and gave a nod. It had been bound to surface and Russ Holt would remember it all well enough.

"Most of us know the truth of things. One last jaunt at a big game might just clear things up all together." Russ gave him a knowing wink. "Knee still pains you then?"

A big pot gone bad, his card sharp rival pulling a gun and leaving him a split-second decision to take the man's life. At the same time a bullet shredding his knee and the woman he'd loved making off with the town's money. Some had blamed him but his leg would never let him forget. "Yep."

"A town like Wylder's apt to excuse a great deal

for a big game filtering in a pretty penny. Give it some thought." Russ smiled and winked. "Welcome home, Dalton."

He tipped his hat and headed back out to the streets of Wylder. He might have figured Sonny's plan before he'd even sought the man out, but he had no intentions of a game. He was too damn tired for more of the same and even with a few days on his father's homestead, he'd found the peace and quiet something he'd almost forgotten could exist. He tucked his cane into the side of the saddle on Sable and giving the horse a pat, mounted up, turning the animal toward…home.

Chapter Three

The afternoon sun let up as Leona trotted down the steps in back of the Vincent House Hotel. She gave a once-over to the darkening sky. Rain was coming with the bit of light wind and hanging clouds. Her Pa used to say he could smell the rain and she inhaled as she headed back to the dress shop. She scrutinized the pouch of money she'd picked up at the hotel. Payment from several customers who had left their clothing for the wash.

She trotted across the street to get ahead of a small carriage. As it passed, she stepped ahead. Out of nowhere a boy grabbed the pouch of money and ran. Leona took off after him running as fast as she could in the wake of his dust. She couldn't let him take the widow's money or she'd never hear the end of it. As they turned the corner, the boy slid in gravel and she grabbed him and then the small bag of money, both of them falling to the ground.

"You no good scoundrel. I'll fix you ya' no good varmint." Leona wrestled with him over the hold on the money, but then he let go.

He tried to scramble from her, but she planted a hand into his hair and twisted, causing him a squalling yelp.

She gained the money and kept him from escaping by the grip she pulled tighter, continuing to wrestle with him as she got them to their feet. "Nothing but a dad-burn boy."

Two large hands eased her aside and grabbed the boy by the ear. He screeched and curled upward on his tip-toes.

"Just what's going on here?" Dalton Payne, the gambler, looked from her to the kid, holding them apart.

Leona lunged for the boy once more, kicking, though the gambler held her back.

"He's a pick pocket what's a goin' on." She tried once more to reach for the thief who might have been all of twelve. "I'll teach the weasel somethin' bout thief'in. Let me at 'em." She fought to free Dalton's grip from her upper arm.

"You stand right here and don't move, not an inch." His deep green eyes bore down on her as he let her go pointing at her. "Not another word."

Her mouth fell open at his scolding and she folded her arms, gritting her teeth.

He grabbed the boy by the arm, turning loose his ear. "Gideon, what've you to say for yourself, huh?"

The boy shrugged away, lifting the biggest blue eyes Leona had ever seen, the scraggily looking runt. At least she had the Widow Lowery's money back. Any fight was far better than explaining lost money to the dress shop owner if it came down to it.

"I told you, boy, you had choices when you got off that train. Didn't I?" He scolded the boy. And how did he know this thieving kid anyway?

Gideon gave a slight nod and wiped the blood from his lip. Well, at least she'd belted him one good one he'd deserved!

"Look at me. You're trying to steal this woman's money?" He shifted his weight, holding the boy's gaze with the question.

The boy backed up a step. "Thought she was a kid like me. She ain't lookin' much like a woman dressed like that anyways."

Dalton grabbed his ear again and he howled. "You will apologize to the lady, not give your opinion."

"Sorry, Ma'am. Sorry, let me go." The boy rubbed his ear as Dalton turned him loose.

"You're gonna get yourself shot or worse. Why aren't you heeding my advice?" Dalton's voice dropped an octave, his brows knitted tight.

Gideon eyed her again and then looked at Dalton. "I tried what you said and ain't nobody a gonna hire me for nothin' other than shoveling manure, but they ain't a payin' much for that neither."

Dalton bent to lift his cane from the ground and studied the boy for a long moment. "You know anything about plowing with a mule?"

The youth nodded with a shrug. "Sure. Don't everybody?"

"Good. Then you be at my homestead, the old Payne place, just north of town, by six come morning. I'll pay you a fair day's wages for working for me. Be on time or don't come." The gambler reached into his pocket and drew out three coins, giving them to the lad.

Leona's slammed her hands to her hips. What was he doing giving that thieving kid money and work?

"Get yourself something to eat and head on to my homestead tonight. You can sleep in the barn loft. Think you can find it?" Dalton asked, leaning on his cane.

Gideon picked up his hat staying shy of Leona as he walked away from them both, glancing back once. "I can find it, all right."

"You just gonna give him money and let him go, the weasel?" Leona shouted so the boy would hear her.

He turned back to her. "Look, he was on the train when I came in. Not a very good pick pocket which tells me a couple of things."

She scowled, miffed if nothing else. "Like what? A mule shittin' thief?"

"One, he's not a thief by nature and two he's hungry. A person will do almost anything when his belly's empty." He tilted his hat back taking a long hard look at her. "And what about you?"

Leona picked her up her hat and plopped it on her head. "What about'n me?"

"First off, I had him apologize to a lady, not one who talks like that. And look at you?" He observed her head to toe, making her a bit self-conscious.

"What a ya' mean?" She let her mouth fall open in defense.

"I mean, the boy's right, what's a beautiful young woman like yourself doing wearing men's clothing three times too big for her?" He waited, though the edge of his lips curled into a smile.

"Well…I wear what I have." She didn't dress like a lady often at all, but she worked around boiling pots all day long. Long skirts and all could be dangerous around the flames if they trailed the ground. Besides, the several times she did wear the dress Laurel had given to her to church, the men and even women had mocked and made fun of her. She supposed it was her father's doing. He hadn't known how to teach her to be a lady

26

and she walked and talked a lot like he had always done. And dresses were uncomfortable and itchy and running in a dress was near impossible. It had been the same long ago when her Pa had bought her a new dress for school. The boys had teased her without mercy for weeks simply because they'd never much seen her wear anything but trousers and big shirts. And who was he to be judging her?

"Makes a man like me wonder why you hide like that when you've got about the prettiest amber eyes I've ever seen." He didn't laugh or mock, but instead held her gaze as if he were sincere.

Did he *really* say she was beautiful? And if he did what did that mean? Nope, men didn't think that way about her. Why would this one be any different? "Gambler you ain't funnin' me, are you?"

"No, I'm not funning you." He smiled but then let it fade. "But I tell ya'. I'd like to see you take a little pride in your appearance. Let the people of this town see the real Leona Fabray. Act like the lady I know you can be. And maybe watch that mouth of yours?"

She squinted as he touched her, brushing a gentle thumb across her swollen cheek. Her vision was blurred from the continued tearing of one eye. "What're you a doin?"

"You've dirt on your face and a puffy lip. Come on." He nodded for her to follow.

"Where?" She let him lead her to the bench that sat outside of Jake's Place. The small restaurant held a few patrons enjoying their meals inside.

"Sit." He tugged at her elbow, and she found the bench, sitting. He ran inside the restaurant and then returned, placing a cool rag to her cheek. "Did he hit

27

you?"

"No, got it in the scuffle, I reckon." She shivered at his touch. "You know that boy, Gideon, then?"

"From the train, like I said." He was so close to her she was caught off guard at how handsome he was. He had to be a good bit older than her twenty-two years. His dark beard and his chiseled cheekbones accented the depth of his green eyes….and…she glanced away and then back. She wasn't sure why when she looked at him she kept catching herself staring. He was handsome, but even though he seemed sincere, she couldn't be sure.

"What's a makin' you being so kind to me and him?" She whispered, taken aback by his kindness and the gentleness at which he continued with the cloth. She hadn't even known she was hurt, though the puffiness at her top lip tightened.

He shrugged, still holding the cloth to her chin now. "This world's already got enough bad in it, seems to me nice words of advice and caring for people can go a long way."

Why did her insides flutter like someone had turned loose a barrel of butterflies? And how could a man as handsome as him care about her? "Advice?"

He touched the cool rag to her lip. He smiled, dimples sinking into his cheeks. "You work hard at the dress shop. The widow has a nice place of business there. Add a little pride to your appearance. A blouse and skirt. And brush out this mop of hair." He placed his fingers through length of her hair. "I'd imagine it's beautiful when you've taken time to it."

"You're a funnin' me gambler.' She took the rag for herself, leaning away from him. "I ain't too trusting of a man carrying them fancy words." No man had ever been this nice to her, save Pa. Why did a man like him give two cents at how she dressed or talked?

"Nope, I'm not funning you in the least." He eased up, grabbing his walking stick and holding out a hand to assist her up.

She hesitated and took his hand, warmth surging through her as she got to her feet. His hand was so much larger than her own and while she let go, something inside her didn't want to.

He turned and began walking away leaning on his cane.

"You hurt that leg pulling me and that Gideon apart." She caught up with him, not sure why she followed.

He adjusted his hat, glancing at the darkening sky and then to her. "It'll hurt no matter."

"Gambler how do you know Gideon's gonna show tomorrow?" She asked as she waited, needing to get back to the dress shop before the Widow had a fit.

He took a few more steps, stopped and turned to face her. "I don't. But you bring Ernest. You might just be surprised."

Leona touched her pocket for the widow's money pouch and turned to cross the street. "Then why'd you do it, not knowing if'n he'll show?"

He adjusted his hat staring at her for a long moment. "For the same reason I'll bet on seeing you in new women's clothing coming up real soon." With that he winked at her and turned the corner, laughter echoing in his wake.

"Huh. I ain't wearin' no dressy woman clothes nothing." She shook her head, talking to herself as she met the wash pots once more. What on earth did he see that she'd never found in herself? There was no doubt he was funnin' her like other men had done in the past.

But as she bent to pick up the scrub board the thought struck her. What if he wasn't?

****

Dalton sat on the steps of the porch. He sipped black coffee, adjusting his knee. Some days were harder than others, but as usual he'd work through it, what other choice did he have? But it was nice to be among his father's things. He'd worn one of his father's shirts, the two like in size and he's used his father's old black skillet for preparing breakfast. Though as it was maybe he'd never have a peace about not coming home long before now. His father should have not died alone and he should have come home to spend more time.

The sun had not yet shown itself, but the sky began to reveal colors in the distance. He glanced down the dirt road toward town, looking for Leona who he expected would be on time with Ernest. Gideon had slept in the barn last night. He hadn't made it easy on the boy by checking on him or providing any comforts. If he was gonna hang around then he'd need to earn his keep, better that than stealing it.

It was late summer, so he wouldn't have much of a garden to plow. But he'd need to purchase a couple of oxen come spring. But for now, he'd found an old rusted old plough that belong to his father and with Ernest he could bust up enough ground to plant a few things to keep vegetables on the table.

A rustling sound came from inside the small barn. He chuckled. So Gideon was awake.

"Glad you made it timely." He took a sip of the

black brew and set the mug beside him on the step. Gideon walked toward him, shoving his hands into the pockets of trousers that were a might too short. "There's breakfast inside on the stove. Fill up and we'll see about a good day's work."

He caught the boy's blue-eyed, hesitant gaze. "Go on. Eat. It's all right."

The boy nodded and stepped passed him and into the house without so much as a word. It would take him a bit to trust him he suspected.

He finished the remainder of his coffee and stood without his cane. His knee would ache with or without hard work so he might as well get to it. He turned to head inside when Leona appeared in the distance, riding bareback on the large mule, still dressed in oversized clothing and that floppy brown hat. She was a sight. Some kind of beauty. Thoughts of her had roamed through his mind the night before. The image of what she would look like dressed in fancy clothing had lingered as he'd drifted off to sleep. He wasn't sure why, other than curiosity. Hell, he wasn't being honest with himself. He found her a beauty the likes of which he hadn't seen in a real long time. And she was sincere in who she was and not so caught up about what others thought, though she did need to think about her appearance more. But what business did he have with her other than the mule?

Had he shocked her by telling her she was hiding behind those baggy clothes? Maybe it was time someone did. It had been her eyes that had caught his attention first, the day his black shiny boots had gotten soaked. They were a deep amber, like the warm sun of autumn that rode the sky in the evenings, almost as if they held a fire. Something inside him softened when around her, a place inside his chest he'd ignored for a long time. He'd come home to Wylder to work and settle to a quiet life. He didn't want or need a woman to tangle his thoughts, much less one that would fight in the middle of the street and had a mouth as big as Texas.

"Well, I got on my same old clothes, but I see you're all gussied up for a hard day at the plow." She slid from Ernest and walked toward him.

He regarded the leather work boots he'd purchased at the mercantile, along with brown trousers, suspenders and a soft blue shirt. "Better than my best suit out here."

She gave the mule a pat as she spoke again. "Gonna be a hot 'un today. Make sure you water him good now and at noon. And mind you give him a rest when you take one."

He nodded. "Got it. You hungry? There's a little breakfast inside. Biscuits and beef gravy."

"Nope. Done ate but thank ya' kindly." Gideon stepped outside and her eyes narrowed at the sight of the boy.

She walked closer to the porch, pointing her finger at the boy. "Never thought you'd show. Better watch letting that little bandit into your home."

"I said I was sorry, Ma'am." Gideon backed up a step, keeping Dalton between them. "I ain't a taking nothin'."

"Oh, the sweet act ain't a workin' on me." She put her hands to her hips.

"All right, you two." Dalton took Ernest by the reins, lining up to ride.

"Wait, he'll need ta' get used to you a bit." She warned, her tone alarming.

But he swung a leg over the animal with little effort "I've a way with animals. See? He likes me." He smiled and in the same moment Ernest decided different and took off running. Dalton held onto the reins, but the mule stopped in his tracks, sending him to the ground with a loud thud and a cloud of dust.

"Son of a ...." He coughed, tasting dirt and then gulped for air. After a moment he got himself to standing, hopping with his knee. Damn, but the mule hadn't given much warning about it. He coughed and brushed his clothing.

"Gambler, I told you he ain't the kinda mule that likes all." Leona grabbed Ernest by the reins again.

"Ahh, I planned about getting dirty today. Guess I'm getting' a head start." He could damn well feel his knee. He leaned down and gave it a tender rub but then Gideon giggled.

He glared at the boy, while Leona joined in another bought of laughter.

"Glad I could make it amusing for you both this morning." He hopped around until he worked the kink out of his knee. "I was gonna ride him to the field, then plow. Here you ride, boy."

Gideon took Ernest by the reins, leading the mule a wide berth passed Leona. "Everyone knows ya' can't ride a stubborn mule."

Dalton limped back toward Leona. "I'll have Ernest back tonight, as good as he is now."

She folded her arms. "You injured that knee of yours again, Gambler?"

"It's hurt for so long it's part of me. More pain or

less makes little difference I guess." He'd learned for years to push the ache away, but there were nights it kept him awake. This night would be no different than the rest.

She gave the pout he'd come to find so enticing. "What d'ya do to that knee anyway?"

He sucked in a deep breath and gave her the short version of the answer. "A bad game a long time ago. Best left in the past."

"Well then, I'm off to visit at the Holt ranch for a bit." She adjusted the bag across her shoulder.

"Holt ranch?" He supposed she'd know many of the families in town that he remembered as well.

"Laurel Holt's been teaching me to sew, *like a lady*." She smirked with a lift of her brows. "But I reckon she and the other ladies like the cookies I bring each week. There's me and Laurel, Sarah Taylor and Eliza Jane Sullivan, the Doc's wife, who meet to sew each week." She pulled a paper sack out of her bag and handed it to him. "Here, I made a couple for you and that mongrel of a kid. Mind you he doesn't steal Ernest while you ain't a lookin'."

He accepted the sack. "I'm sure we'll make good use of these. Russ Holt told me Caleb had married, but I assume Daniel went and did the same?"

"Yep, Sarah's a married to Daniel for a bit now." She backed up a step. "Expecting too."

"They were just boys when I left here, now he and Caleb are married. Makes a man feel his age I reckon. Met the new doc in town too." He set the sack on the porch and gave his knee a quick rub before turning to walk back to her.

"My Pa said you're as old as you feel." She

shrugged and eased another hint away from him.

"Well, with this knee I'm about a hundred and three, otherwise…young as needed for this day of work." He turned back to her. The treats were nice and she was learning to sew. And in the early morning sun, he found himself caught up in the features of her face. High arched dark brows, rounded cheeks and full lips. Damnit he knew better than to think that way. Women complicated a lot of things.

"So, if you're learning to sew, gonna change up how you dress a bit then?" He let a smile cross his face, stepping closer, teasing in spite of his thoughts.

She narrowed her gaze, and then the hint of an amused smile lit her face. "Gambler?"

He waited on what she was going to say next, with that big mouth of words she often spit right out.

"You're a standing in poo." She gave a loud snort and moseyed back the way she'd come.

He sized-up his new work boot, stuck in a steaming pile from Ernest. He held a curse as he watched her walk back down the road still giggling, and leaving him to his work and his aching knee.

Chapter Four

Leona drew the last stitch through the material she'd cut and measured. Her very own pattern and creation. She beamed at Laurel. "All finished a 'lessen you can find a poorly sewn stitch somewhere."

"Well…" Laurel took the blouse from her and inspected the seams inside and out. "This is very neat work, Leona."

She'd been working on that blouse and a fine skirt for a few weeks, but this was the first time she'd done it all herself. Not that she'd ever wear them anywhere much.

Sarah continued to embroider a heavy silk scarf. "It's a beautiful blouse, Leona, and the skirt too."

Eliza Jane leaned over where Laurel was sitting to inspect the blouse along with the other ladies. "Leona, you've outdone yourself on these, they are very lovely."

"Thank ya'." She replied, a hint of pride flowing through her.

"The stitching is nice and tight. I'm so proud of you." Laurel gave her shoulder a squeeze. "You're such a fast learner. Maybe Widow Lowery will begin to let you have some of the smaller jobs to help her out since I will miss some time when the baby comes.

"I ain't so sure. I think she likes me at the pots better." Leona added folding her blouse and smoothing the material. "But with Mary picking up the slack maybe one day. Work's been heavy of late and Widow ain't able to help as much."

"I'm afraid the heat gets to her these days." Sarah shook her head and pulled a stitch through.

"I don't mind so much for now. But I'd sure like inside work away from those pots one of these summers." She took the blouse back from Laurel and looked it over again.

"Mama...cookie." Jesse, Laurel's son of three, came running inside, his rooster, Harold, close on his heels. "Harold need a cookie too."

Laurel handed her son a cookie from the bag Leona had brought. "One for you. I'll save the crumbles for Harold for later." Jesse scampered back out to the porch, the small rooster following along.

"Awe, he's growing so fast." Sarah set her stitching aside in her lap admiring. She rested a hand on her own belly.

"Yes, well Jesse is a handful and we mustn't forget Harold." Laurel peered outside to keep an eye on her son.

"That rooster still follows him everywhere." Leona chuckled as the boy and rooster went back outside.

"I make him put Harold in his pen at night these days. Jesse wants him on his bed when it's time to sleep." Laurel giggled. "It's sweet, but enough is enough and with another on the way."

"How are you feeling Laurel?" Sarah asked, adding a smile.

"I feel well except mornings. Doc Sullivan says things are fine. But Caleb won't let me do a thing...which is kind of nice. He is so very excited about the baby, insisting it's a girl this time." Laurel rubbed her extended belly.

"Well, it's exciting times." Leona smoothed and folded a new piece of taffeta material she planned to use for a skirt.

Laurel walked to the window to gaze out at Jesse once more. "Leona, you didn't ride Ernest today?"

"Nope, I left him at the Payne homestead. That gambler fella wanted to use Ernest to plow up a small garden. But Ernest threw him this morning. I tried to tell him, but you know men ain't so good at listening. He wasn't hurt none, 'ceptin he's got a bad knee of sorts anyway." Leona nibbled at one of the cookies.

"Caleb mentioned Mr. Payne had returned to town." Laurel took her place on the settee once more. "Says he left here a long time ago. All the men in town are hoping he'll want to set up a big poker championship to make money for the township."

Sarah lifted her embroidery again. "Daniel said the same, though he's not much for gambling when it comes down to it. Thinks it will bring more ruffians to town."

Eliza Jane nodded. "Sam met him; and said he was as nice a man, just like his father. But imagine that, a famous gambler returned home to Wylder. You know I read in the paper where he even played a tournament with President Grant some time back."

"Uncle Russ says if Mr. Payne can be talked into participating it would be very big indeed." Laurel added as she lifted her sewing again.

"Russ had better watch himself," Eliza Jane chirped. "Mother is tiring of him hanging around that saloon so much."

"He ain't playin', the gambler I mean, least he says

he ain't. He came to retire and work the land, though he ain't a showing me much with Ernest tossing him a head over heels." Leona narrowed her gaze to all the woman looking at her. "What? Y'all look like the cat done held your tongue for ya'. Well, at least he told me he's retired once and for all. He even turned down Sonny Cash in planning the whole thing. I think he's more interested in just settling in on his Pa's old homestead and plantin' that late garden."

"You seem to know quite a bit about Mr. Payne." Laurel lifted her brows in question.

Eliza Jane set her sewing aside and waited, as did Sarah. "Do tell us."

"Y'all ain't a fair bunch," Leona chided, standing and folding the blouse along with the skirt into her bag. "It ain't like that at all. Besides I wouldn't know what to do with a man anyway and y'all all three married women know that. I just ain't meant for such." She sat once more in a huff.

Laurel scooted closer. "I'm teasing but you mind to be careful. A gambler and all. Even though Caleb and Russ speak highly of him."

"But the scandal when he left," Sarah took up her embroidery again. "Daniel said he never had a chance, the fight he got in was over a woman and she made off with the town's money. She shot him in the knee and never looked back, so he left town for good they say."

Leona had heard the story, but she hadn't known the part about it being a woman who took the town's money. "Well, he's a very kind man, seems to care for people in general, least wise he didn't yell at me when I dumped water all over his boots. He's a looking after a boy named Gideon, who bounced off the train a pic

39

pocket. He's making him work for his money now. It's his mission to help I reckon."

"All right, y'all can get over yourn gawking. There ain't, nothing to tell except we done a little talking over his soggy boots and his using Ernest." Leona folded her arms with a pout.

Laurel tipped her head, studying her. "Leona, do you know how...well, how things happen between a man and woman?"

Leona frowned, "Why you askin' me what I don't know, 'stead of what I do?"

"I know you lost your mother at such a tender age. I suppose I just...want you to know to talk to us should you have questions, in making such a quick...friend with Mr. Payne." Laurel glanced to the other women, who nodded their agreement.

"Well, I did see one of the whores in the alley with a miner once. Walked right up on 'em with him a gruntin' and ruttin, both as naked as jaybirds. I seen animals too, so I can guess it similar. If'n I ever need some advice, I'll ask." Her face heated. She knew nothing much about it at all. Why did women carry on so about it anyway? Seemed to her it wasn't nothing but a big dirty play on groping a woman's private parts.

Laurel placed her hand on Leona's. "But what you saw in the alley isn't how things are when you...love a husband. It can be very nice when.... oh lands. I am blushing.... but when you love or you're in love it is a very nice thing for a man and woman to share, or at least it can be."

"All my ma ever told me was it hurts and to run from any man who tries, said if I keep a penny held between my knees was the best plan." She shrugged, remembering the sounds that came from her parents' room long ago.

Sarah giggled, and looped another thread through her work. "Well, that's not bad advice until you are in love and ready to marry."

"I supposin' ain't no man interested no way, ceptin' the gambler said he'd like to see me a wearin' stuff like I'm a sewing. Ladies' dresses and such." She could still hear Dalton's voice and her heart beat faster in remembering. "And he, well he said that I had beautiful eyes and he likes my hair is all. I think maybe he's just funnin' me."

Laurel held a hand to her mouth and stifled a giggle. "You know what I think? Leona, if you wore these new clothes and put your hair up. It might just turn his head enough to see what he is thinking."

Sarah pulled more thread through the material. "He's a bit older though, isn't he?"

"I figure him for nearing forty. But he's a might handsome when he's all gussied up in his black suit and gray vest and that dark hair… but he has the greenest eyes I've ever seen." She stated it faster than her mind caught on that all the ladies were now eyeing her even closer. Heat rushed her cheeks, but she went on anyway. "Every time I done worn pretty clothes, men and even the ladies make a mockery of me, so I ain't a too fond about it."

Laurel glanced at the other ladies, touching her hand. "Seems to me perhaps you might want to wear that blouse and skirt very soon then. I don't suspect he is funning. as you say, men aren't often to speak of such things unless serious about them."

"Nahh. It's not like that...think he's just trying to

keep me out of trouble, cause I gave a good whippin' to that Gideon when he tried to take the money pouch." Leona didn't think he was smitten, but as for her, she'd had a hard time of keeping her mind from the man and she hadn't understood it a bit.

Her friends exchanged glances, and she shook her head at their continued display.

"Well, I'd know if there's a somethin' more and you'd all be the first I'd tell. But stop a gawking at me 'till there's a something to see...we got sewing to learn me." She took up another piece of linen, determined not to saying another word where Dalton Payne was concerned.

****

Dalton removed his shirt and began washing up at the outside pump. Gideon had worked to add a new handle to the pump and had gotten the rusty metal working once more. The boy had surprised him by doing a decent day's work behind the mule, teaching him a thing or two he'd forgotten from his own youth.

Gideon stopped Ernest beside him, wiping his brow with a sleeve.

"Son, I thank you for a good day's work. With this knee of mine, I'd never make the kind of progress we have." He pooled water in his hand and drank. "Get that shirt off and wash up and we'll see about some supper."

The boy hesitated but began rolling up his sleeves and unbuttoned the two top buttons on his shirt.

"Come on, boy, we both smell as bad as Ernest." He touched Gideon's collar, but he jerked free, stepping away. But not before Dalton caught a glimpse of the scars across his shoulders and back.

"Who put those marks on you?" He lowered his

tone, though rage tore through him to think someone had left scars like that on a child.

The boy shrugged. "Don't matter much now, it was a long time ago."

"If you and I are gonna work together on this homestead, we have to be able to talk, son." He stepped closer, holding the boy's stare.

Gideon began pulling the pump and washed his arms and said no more.

He looked on as the boy did the best he could to wash without removing his shirt. He supposed he'd discovered too much, but enough to understand why the boy was on his own. He'd never been one to think a child deserved a strap that drew blood.

"You won't ever get a whippin' here, but we do have to talk about a few details. Your pay and living here." He drew his shirt back on, trying to find the right words.

"No, Sir...I've...well, if I could just eat, I'd be obliged." He scratched his shaggy head, waiting. "Don't mind the work for eatin'."

He studied the boy for a moment. He must have been through hell to be on the run from being beaten and then near starving to boot. "You work an honest day like today. You keep working for me and we'll both eat well, but, I've a spare room inside, two small beds there. If you're not opposed you can sleep there instead of the loft. And I'll pay you fair as long as you stay out of trouble."

Gideon's brows lifted. "Ain't slept in a real bed in a long time."

"As long as you promise no picking pockets, you'll have a bed and money." He smiled and if he wasn't mistaken the boy did too, though he still stared at the ground.

"I's just gonna take enough to eat and then when I got work pay Miss Leona back. Like that lady on the train, but she grabbed my hair and... you won't believe me anyway...though." Gideon's shook his head.

"Try me. What about the lady on the train?" He asked, curious, if nothing else and began to work the buttons of his shirt.

The boy kicked at the dirt. "I thought if'n I had her pouch of coins I could follow her where she went in town and tell her I found it left on the train. Best I figured she might've given me a coin or two to eat on for a few days. And Miss Leona, I just thought I could grab a few coins and toss it back to her, but she punched and pulled my hair like some wild cat."

He had to hide a grin. She was that. "Well, I'm coming to figure Miss Leona a spitfire too, be good to Ernest as you have been, and you might win her over."

"Might be best I stay away from her for a while." Gideon shrugged and pushed Ernest back.

Dalton laughed. "What about school?"

The boy lifted his head to reveal dirt smudged across his chin. "I ain't been in a long time, but I can sypher figures and read well enough."

He nodded, tucking in the tails of his shirt. "Maybe we should see about getting you registered for the school in town, you can help me with chores evenings and Saturdays, but your learning's important."

The boy was already shaking his head. "Ain't no need for school anymore if I'm a working man."

Maybe now wasn't the time but he'd work on the kid little by little. "I've gotta run the mule back to town.

You get cleaned up and have a bit of the stew on the stove. We can talk about school later."

Gideon handed him the reins to Ernest. "Dalton?"

He turned, grabbing his hat again.

The kid hesitated. "I heard the men at the saloon talkin' about how famous you got making money gambling and all, but they said you ain't gonna play no games here. Why not if'n you're that good?"

He let the question run across him. "I'm retired, boy. Gonna work this land. Gonna work you and gonna rest this leg when I can."

"But they said you're the best, sure to win." The kid's blue eyes widened, something like his own use to do.

He laughed out loud. "Pokers just luck, son, and sometimes it's time to let go of luck and make your own way."

"Maybe you can teach me poker then?" He shrugged.

He smiled, then winked. "Doubt it."

Gideon frowned. "All right."

"Dalton?" The boy turned again and sighed. "Why you helping me like you are?"

"Because I've read a lot of faces, and yours told me you weren't a thief." He waited and Gideon smiled and trotted toward the house.

"Gideon?" He called and the boy turned again. "For what it's worth, I do believe you about Leona and the woman on the train."

The boy gave a nod, his blue eyes as true as Dalton already knew them to be.

Chapter Five

The evening sun dropped low behind the trees, leaving scattered shadows along the ground as Leona took the road back toward town. She whistled, carrying the skirt and blouse in the bag over her shoulder, proud that they were now finished to Laurel's full satisfaction. Though she wasn't a planning to wear them any time soon. They'd be uncomfortable at the hot pots she worked and a corset was so off putting she had no idea why women insisted on wearing one.

A snap of twigs turned her. But before she could react, someone grabbed her from behind. Another man emerged before her, his eyes dark and his clothing unkempt. Both had come out of the woods, and were on her so fast there was no time to scream. She fought as they struggled to hold her, the world spinning as she tried to free herself. She scratched and clawed at the hands holding her still.

"Looky what we found, and a mouth on her too." The first man jerked her around to face him. She swung a fist, catching him across the cheek. How had she not been more careful in knowing better than to walk home alone?

"Leave me be, you heaping piles of horse shit." She shoved back at the man before her, punching and managing to slip free for a second before they had her again.

"Girl, we're just getting started. Hit me again sweets and I'll belt you a good one." The first man pulled her close to his face. The lingering smell of whiskey on his breath turned her belly and she pulled away. Her bag fell from her shoulder to the ground. "You'd best be on your way, or you'll get a good fight, toad suckers."

She swung both fists, making contact with a jaw. The man in front of her caught and twisted her wrist until she screamed. She hit him again with her other balled fist several times to no avail. She screamed again.

And then it came, a knee to her belly, doubling her to the ground. She tried to scream but had nothing left but a cough and wheeze. Another fist caught her cheek, snapping her head back. The warm copper taste of blood filled her mouth as she struggled to gain a ragged breath. She was going to pass out…no, she couldn't let them…she had to fight but there was nothing left…

"Hold still little lady and this won't take long at all." The growl of the man's voice was at her ear as he pinned her to the ground, working her legs apart. He slapped her twice more, the impact stunning her to remain still until she understood his intentions.

She balled her fists and slammed both of them into his faced with all the might she could muster, finding a cheek and his ear.

He yelped and fell full on top of her, gripping her breasts as he pressed one arm to the ground. "All right little lady, you like it rough."

No, he couldn't.... no... She swung her fist, aiming for his face. But then he grabbed her shirt and ripped it open baring her breasts.

He cursed with the impact of another hit from her as the second man bent to hold her down, laughing.

The man atop her worked at pulling her pants from her, the struggle frustrating him as she locked her grips to her roped belt.

"Shut up girl, won't take us long to do you." He growled as he fought with the front of his britches.

"No... you no goods, I won't let you...toad suckers touch me." She had no breath and her words were but a whisper. She screamed, as another smack came across her face, blurring her vision. She held a hand to her eye, curling away. At the same time the man on top of her yelped and fell away to the ground.

"You, son of a ...." The man holding her never finished his sentence. Dalton's brass ended cane thumped his head with a thud. He tumbled back from her and moved no more like his friend.

Leona rolled to her side holding her eye, sure she was going to pass out.

Even with her vision blurred she could tell from the tenderness as he gathered her against his chest, it was Dalton who had come. A gentle hand brushed her hair from her face and she held his gaze, confused. She tried to sit but couldn't orient herself through the pain and the dizziness inside her head.

"Leona?" His deep voice came to her as if he was at a distance, but she clung to him holding her shirt closed.

He covered her with his duster and lifted her into his arms. "It's gonna be all right now..."

"Dalton..." She tried to speak. He couldn't carry her with his bad leg, but she hurt and her vision wasn't clear and things were fading around her...

"Shhhh, I've got ya. They won't hurt you anymore." His voice vibrated through her chest with a depth of warmth. And all she could do was grab the front of his shirt to hang on though the world spun her right into the waiting darkness.

****

Dalton made it to the homestead still carrying Leona. She was unconscious but still somehow clung to the front of his shirt. He scrambled up the steps and pushed through the front door, kicking it closed behind him.

Gideon jumped up from the table, his eyes wide as saucers. "What happened?"

"A couple of men roughed her up on the road to town." He eased Leona to his bed, careful to keep his coat across her naked chest. He wasn't sure how bad she might be hurt and there was no time to waste in getting the doctor.

"Boy, you think you can saddle up and ride Sable to town, let the sheriff know to pick up two men on the road outside the Holt ranch?" He placed a palm to Leona's cheek. "Bring the doc back here, too."

"I can ride Sable? Sure, I can do it, easy." Gideon grabbed his hat.

"Go then, don't want them to get away. I tied 'em to each other so they won't be going far. He poured water from the pitcher into the basin and sunk a cloth into the bowl. He eased the cool cloth to the open gash above Leona's eye. He'd see those men did their time and if not he'd take care of that for the sheriff.

Gideon ran out the front door slamming it behind him.

Dalton eased his coat from her and sucked in a

tight breath at the quick view of her pert breasts. He eased her over to her side, finding bruises along her back and shoulders. He cleaned the dirt from her skin, cursing under his breath at what had been done to her.

She whimpered.

"Shhh, it's all right, rest." He rolled her to her back once more, and pulled her boots off, dropping them to the floor. With a bit of hesitation, he tugged her britches away leaving her in long pantaloons. Damn, he gulped hard. She was sure enough a real beauty laying naked in his bed, but he covered her with the quilt, gulping a much-needed breath.

He sat and brushed her hair back and used the cloth to wipe away the dried blood across her cheek and brow.

"Gambler..." She opened one eye to look at him, her voice but a whisper.

"I'm here." He placed the cloth to the cut once more.

"Those men?" She winced but blinked her good eye.

"You won't have to worry about them again. I sent Gideon for the sheriff to pick 'em up. You're safe now." His spoke in a whisper.

"I don't even know where they came from." She touched her brow, but he took her hand back down to the blanket.

"Men like that wait, looking for trouble." He brushed her hair back from her face again. "Leona, they didn't hurt you? I mean...they didn't..." Hell, he didn't think so, but he had to ask.

"No." She wasn't focused well, but she answered. "No, though they were a tryin'...Gambler if you hadn't come along. Ernest?" She fretted, tears streaming her face.

He'd damn well rather take a beating than see a woman in tears, especially her.

"Oh, he's fine, didn't give me a bit if trouble as I carried you back here." He whispered. "Followed me the whole way because I had you."

She moaned, reaching for her back. "My back…. pains where one of 'em kicked me. The bastards…"

"Shhhh, you've some good bruising there, just gonna have to rest, but here…" He lifted his coat and searched in the pocket for the small metal flask of bourbon and eased it to her. "Sip this. Bourbon."

Leona closed her eyes and then blinked several times. "Never drank any spirits a 'fore."

"It'll help you rest." He urged, pushing the flask to her lips. "Sent Gideon for the doc, but this'll help. Come on."

She gulped and frowned, forcing a swallow and then coughed with a heavy wheeze.

"A bit more, it won't help if you don't take enough." He eased the bottle back to her lips, giving her little choice.

"I do hurt so bad…" She sucked down more of the liquor and growled, shaking her head. "That's just awful…"

He capped the small bottle amused. "Let that settle, close your eyes and rest until the doc gets here."

She did as he said, her good eye closing, though she held to his hand. He studied her slight fingers tangled with his own. A warmth he hadn't encountered in a hell of a long time flowed through his chest. And he damn well knew better than to allow those feeling to creep back in.

"Gambler if you hadn't come along. Never been afraid of anything 'till now." She gripped tighter.

"Ahh. You're not afraid of anything, girl." He turned the crank and dimmed the lantern. "They won't hurt you anymore, rest now."

"Gambler?" She let go of his hand.

"Huh?"

"Somebody stripped me naked in this here bed. I ain't gonna ask if'n it was you who went and done that." She blushed an enticing shade of pink.

"Maybe its best you don't ask then." He gave her a wink, but tugged the covers higher.

"I reckon no harm done." She adjusted in the bed with a groan. "Gambler will you sit here tonight with me? Just need to rest, so tired…afraid a bit…"

"I'm not going anywhere, Leona." He brought her hand to his lips, kissing the back.

What a hell of a day. What a hell of an arrival…home. He'd planned to move back for some peace and quiet. Not to get thrown from an angry mule, beat up two no goods, put an injured woman in his bed and besides that take in a boy who had no story to tell…all in a short time. No peace and quiet here.

He studied Leona for a long moment. Even battered and bruised she was something to behold. A spit-fire of feistiness that was rather entertaining if nothing else. He wasn't sure how he was feeling about any of it. She was the first woman in a very long time to turn his head. It didn't make any darn sense, neither of them having nothing in common. So why had she lingered on his mind day and night since his return?

Chapter Six

Leona jolted awake, startled from her sleep over a dream the men were attacking her again. She must have screamed in fright because Dalton was there.

"Hey, just a dream. It's all right." He coaxed, wrapping his arms about her, causing her a deep shiver as the warmth from his naked chest engulfed her.

"But it was so real. Like they had me again." She held him, wanting to never let him go. How had she had such a frightening dream? Those men were not here now and she was aware of that, though she shivered anyway.

He ran a hand through the length of her hair. "They're gone, sheriff turned 'em over to the law in Kansas wanted for rustling and a whole lot of other things."

"Well, they rustled me up again it seems. Maybe I can't ever sleep in peace again, bad dreams an' all." She ignored the pain in her back and leg to keep holding him.

"You will sleep again." He whispered, touching her cheek. "Just give it some time and rest like the doctor said."

"You're so good to me Gambler and I know you didn't plan on this, me being here for a while. I can't even remember how many days I've been laying here, like they all try to run together." When she looked up his green-eyed gaze held her. He did that a lot. Watched her, making her whole-body flush with heat. No man had ever been as good to her save her father.

"It's been about three nights now, four days" He brushed her hair back from her face. "Your eye is looking much better."

"Feels better and my headaches faded. My leg's just sore like my back, but walking with Laurel helped some." She explained as she leaned away from him. It had been so easy to let him hold her and he'd been attentive to her care, but...it wasn't proper, was it? What would the town and even the widow think about her stay here?

"Doc said you could move around as you felt like it, but rest for a week or more." He moved to the chair beside the bed. "Laurel left you a few items, but I'll get you some new clothing from town."

"New clothes? I can just wear my clothes I had, mend my shirt." She eased back into the pillows, tugging the covers higher across her.

"Burned 'em. Ripped up and covered in blood." He wasn't frowning as he said it. "I'll get you some new blouses, skirts and other things you may need."

She folded her arms. "Well, I can't work in no skirt, all gussied up like a girl. Gonna need more pants and regular shirts. Those boilers are hot...wait, why would you do that anyway?"

"Why?" He squinted, angling a hard look at her.

"Yes why?" She pouted. She'd been here a few days now, the first of those days caught up in fitful dreams due to the pain medication the doctor had left for her.

"Because.... I..... I.....Because I think maybe you've

never had the opportunity to wear nice things. Every woman deserves to have pretty dresses and skirts, things to make her feel as beautiful as she is."

"Gambler....you ain't funnin' me?" She couldn't wear a skirt working the pots all day, but what was he saying? He had to be making light of her, didn't he? Most men never paid her any attention at all, so why was he?

"No, I'm not funning you, Leona, not even a little." His narrowed a gaze on her and joined her on the bed, sitting beside her. "Damn it…didn't plan on this, but…"

The light touch of Dalton's soft lips found her own. She didn't move, a shudder running through her entire body as he held the kiss for a long moment, tasting her lips and then parting her mouth to open. His lips were warm and soft, though his beard tickled as he urged her lips to open.

A slight sigh escaped her as if his mouth drew it from the depths of her, but she allowed it. He teased her with his tongue, kissing her with a passion she wasn't sure she understood.

"Does that answer your question?" He asked, his hands resting on her sides. "I've sat here watching you these couple of nights…not sure what the hell I'm doing but I won't tell you I haven't wanted to do that."

"Gambler?" She whispered at his tender words. "I ain't ever been kissed 'till now."

He gave her a soft smile, playing his hand in her hair. "Well, then maybe it's time. I don't know Leona, my thoughts here, been caring for you and all. You know I came back here to make life simple, work the homestead. But having you here, besides your injuries, well…I like it. I like it a lot. I know it doesn't make much sense at all. I'm nearing forty, had a number of women in my life over the years, none that ever turned my head twice, but you…only you, Leona."

"Me?" She whispered, trying to focus on his words as she adjusted in bed once more. Was he in love with her? Had he kissed her and now he was talking love like things to her? No man had ever done that either, but he went on.

"What would you say, if you and I…" He tried again stumbling over his words. "Well, if we did spend some time…together."

She asked, puzzled. "Courtin'?"

"Yep…insane, isn't it?" He held a wide toothy grin. "And why not?"

She was at a loss for words that might have been a first for her. Laurel had been right about his interest of her. "I'd like that Gambler…a whole lot. And to think, it all started with me a pourin' dirty water across them fancy boots of yours."

His lips met hers again in a tender kiss. "You rest like the doc said and I'll see what I can do…about some courting. I suppose I am glad about that water that covered my boots."

"Gambler?" She touched her tingling lips with her fingers. "You've been so many places. There's bound to be a woman or several who caught your fancy, why me? And I don't even know that much about you, 'ceptin you're a kind man."

He took a deep breath and sat beside her on the bed yet again. "Leona, I have been all around, and I'll never lie to you that there was a woman or two in my past. Almost got married once, but she blew out this knee --

that's a story for another time."

He reached and took her hand in his own, studying it as if he were reading a book. "But I have nothing to hide, nothing I can't tell you. I've made my living at the tables, earned more than we could ever spend in a lifetime. Played with the best and lost to a lot of them. Won more than I ever thought possible."

He hesitated but then chuckled. "Played with President Grant once and beat the pants right off him, but he was amused by that. Bought me a drink. Played in ballrooms with chandeliers and in casinos built on the coast, seen a lot of things and a whole heck of a lot of people. I'm set in my ways I suppose."

"But we don't even know much about each other, like you don't even know I lost my Mama when I'z ten and my Pa done raised me alone. He'd be why I like my britches and my big shirts; guess he didn't know how to raise no girl." She shrugged and fidgeted with the covers. "He's a good Pa though, loved me so much, but he got sick and I've been on my own ever since, hadn't any other choice I reckon. We had no other family, a grandma who died long a'fore I can remember. But if you are playin' with me gambler, I ain't got much fight right now, but I will."

"Leona, I'm being sincere. That's a hard life you've had, but you asked me why you?" The edges of his lips curled. "What do you see when you look at yourself?"

She frowned. "Guess I'm just a spinster tomboy, as most folks might agree. My Pa always said I was a little rough around the edges is all."

"You know what I see?" He touched her hair again. "A beauty who doesn't even know it. A woman who takes care of herself, has dreams, like seeing the ocean, but accepts people for who they are. And for reasons I am not sure I can explain, I find myself comfortable with you. I'm sorry those men hurt you, but having you here, well, I'm not sorry at all about that. It makes this house feel like a home and I haven't had a home for a long time."

"Well, that's good but I go home soon." She reminded him, though it wasn't her home she was longing for. He was somehow a comfort of which she had never expected. "Gambler, I felt that comfort too when you carried me back here. I hung onto you as tight as I could."

"I came back here to leave the poker behind, just work the land a bit, sit by the fire evenings, but I never expected you." He took her hand and studied it in his own. "Not sure I am so good for any promises, but what do you say we work on it?"

She held his deep green eyes, and it was as if her heart fluttered with his continued stare. "All right, I'd like that."

He kissed her hand and let go winking at her before making his way from the room.

She touched the tenderness he'd left behind along her lips with her fingers. He'd smelled nice, clean like soap and his mouth on hers had been awkward, though it had sparked a yearning deep in side of her.

She settled back into the covers and smiled. "Well, Leona I reckon you've gone and got yourself a beau."

****

It was after dark as Dalton closed the barn doors, leaving Sable and Ernest with their oats and a new trough of water. He took in the setting sky, the oranges of the leftover sun, leaving streaks like fine cotton in rows. What the he'll was he doing? He hadn't let a woman; any woman get under his skins for a lot of years now. And Leona for reasons he wasn't sure about had slipped right inside the center of his chest. As easy as that.

She was tough as nails and he suspected those two men had found that out for themselves with the fight she gave them. But he'd had no business in kissing her like he had moments ago. She'd been so soft spoken and beautiful in spite of her injuries. And he'd done it with the ease with which he took each breath.

He gave a heavy sigh. He hadn't come home to Wylder for all this, a wayward kid who needed a home and a tomboy wash woman who had a mouth on her. But here he was and somehow it was…maybe just what he needed. Maybe even perfect.

And while he'd never allowed himself the liberty of thinking about having a family, he'd never expected Leona. At first, he'd been caught up in her beauty, something she hid behind that floppy hat. Hell, she had no idea how beautiful a woman she was and that intrigued him the most.

He was a might older than her, nearing forty to her twenty-two years. He'd though himself well past the idea of a wife or even a family, but whenever he was around Leona the thought tugged at him. She was not as some thought, a simple woman, she was anything but, smarter than most women he'd encountered. And she lived each day as it came her except where the wash was concerned. She was comfortable even if it made no sense at all and now, he'd kissed her and he damn well wanted to do that again. So be it. Nothing in his whole life had ever made any sense until now...until Leona.

He went back inside to check on her, the kid still finishing up the dishes. He opened the door to find Leona sleeping and walked closer.

He touched a strand of her long dark hair. And whose business would it be anyway should a crazy old gambler fall for the likes of a baggy clothed beauty with a big mouth? Well, he was gonna remedy that baggy clothing with a few extravagant gowns and some blouses and pants for better working around the pots she heated. And maybe he was gonna see what the rest of his life looked like with her....and the kid given a bit of time.

He made his way back outside to the front porch to sit and rest his leg.

"I'm heading to bed, tired." Gideon joined him on the porch.

"Goodnight, Gideon." He glanced back at the boy and turned to face the night once more. Those words, the ones families said to each other weren't to be taken for granted.

The door crept back open and he glanced back as Leona, wrapped in a blanket, walked closer.

"You shouldn't be out here..." He took the hand she held out and she took her time to sit beside him with care.

"Oh, I'm a gonna live." She tugged the blanket around her and leaned into him. "Saw you watching the sun setting and I thought I could see it too."

He wrapped an arm around her. "I was just thinking about you."

"You were?" She giggled and rocked into him.

"Yep, but you should be resting." He took in a

deep breath and let it out. The hint of lilac in her hair enticing him to breathe again.

"I can rest in a bit." She didn't move but watched the sky before her.

He did the same, no words needed, no hopes but one moment or one day at a time. Content was what he was, very content. No rush to this or that, just day to day, evening to evening and so on.

"Gambler?" She whispered though she didn't look at him. "You think we gone and got love somehow?"

He waited to answer for a long moment. "Is that how you'd really like things, Leona?"

"Sure, think so."

"Then we'll call it that if you like." He found her hand beneath the blanket and brought it to his lips.

"I knew you were a good man, Gambler, when I first poured that water across your boots and you didn't haul off a swinging and a swearing." She gave his hand a squeeze.

"Oh, I can come up with a bit of swearing when needed." He laughed, "And if I know anything about it, you might just out do me there."

She gave him a nudge. "Well, seems I've had to fight for everything so hard my whole life and all, thinking about a home with you when the time is right, well, it seems right peaceful."

He hugged her tighter and watched the sky once more, pondering all life might hold if he played his cards right this time. "That is does."

****

The town of Wylder was busy under the early afternoon sky. Dalton tossed a new plow and a pile of leather harnesses into the back of the small wagon that had belonged to his father. He'd had to repair a couple of spokes in one wheel but Ernest had pulled it along with ease. The wagon was now filled with the shingles for the new barn roof and he had plans to start on that soon enough with Gideon's help.

The kid sat on the buckboard and Dalton had come to enjoy the company the boy had become as they worked together.

Dalton glanced at the boy who was watching two men ride through with fancy horses. He'd feel better about it though if he knew the boy's story and could get him back in school. Gideon was smart and schooling would take him further to being the kind of man he should be one day. But he had to take it a step at a time and earn more of the kid's trust.

"Seems we've a score to settle, Payne." A man in a dark suit stepped up.

Dalton rested his hand on the revolver at his hip.

"Oh, no need to reach for your weapon, Payne. Our settlement will come at the table." Lefty Pearson, moved closer, tilting his hat back. How the hell was he still alive?

"Thought you might've met your end by now, Lefty." He narrowed his gaze on the card cheat. He'd beaten the man in five card draw in Kansas, leaving him broke and that wasn't the first time they'd crossed paths over the years.

The man laughed in a growl. "They want a game here, and most are sayin' you aren't buying in. Looks like you'd want the chance of clearing your name, giving me a bid at gaining my money back."

The man folded his arms. Lefty was no real threat, a big mouth who was no good at poker.

"I'm retired now. I'll leave the cheatin' to you, Lefty. Have yourself a good day." He angled a hard glance at the man.

Pearson's brows narrowed. "Never figured you much for a coward...till now."

"Whip is ass, Dalton." Gideon stood on the buckboard, in defense, surprising him.

Pearson nodded towards Gideon. "Whatcha' pickin' up strays these days, Payne? Best take a strap to control that kid if he's yourn."

Before Dalton could move, Gideon sprang down from the wagon. "I ain't no stray you bastard and no one's lickin' me either."

The kid made a lunge, but he grabbed him by the belt, stopping him in his tracks. "Get in the wagon. Now!"

Gideon glared at the man but did as he was told, his face red and angry as he climbed back up.

Dalton turned back to Lefty. "You know, Pearson, I've a good mind to turn this kid loose and let him whip you a good one, but seeing we've got all these people watching, how about you go find yourself a nice table to cheat."

Pearson tipped his hat, glancing at the gathered crowd. "Until the game, Payne, until the game."

Dalton set his cane inside the buckboard and climbed up beside Gideon who sulked, arms folded. He clucked his tongue and Ernest moved the wagon along. It wasn't until they were clear of town that he noticed Gideon's tears.

"You should have let me at him." Gideon gripped his palms into fists, gritting his teeth. "And he called you a coward, why didn't you fight him, right there, just like that?"

He pulled Ernest to a stop. "First, not everyone is worth the fight. Remember that. Now I know I'm not your father, Gideon, but you watch that mouth of yours too. Curses coming from a boy like you don't sound nice at all."

"But he ain't got no right callin' me no stray or you a coward." Gideon brushed a sleeve across his face. "Like I ain't ever belonged nowhere anyway…" He jumped from the wagon and took off. Ernest bucked, jostling the wagon.

"Whoa, Ernest. Whoa. Gideon, wait." Dalton shouted, holding the reins tighter, but Gideon was gone.

In minutes, he'd managed to get Ernest back to the homestead. He didn't figure Gideon to run anywhere else or maybe the stream where he liked to fish evenings. He eyed the barn where the door was ajar. He ambled there and went inside waiting. And then it came; a sniffle from the loft.

He took a deep breath and let it out. "I uh, figured you might be here. I'm not so sure why you got upset but I'm here to listen."

"Well, I ain't just trash or a stray dog like he said." Gideon's voice was muffled. "And you ain't no coward, neither."

"Name callings just what it is. Not worth the worry it's given." He glanced up again, where a trickle of hay fell through the parted boards.

"It's worth it to me." Gideons voice rose an octave.

He leaned against the ladder. "My legs not gonna let me climb up. Care to come down?"

A moment later, Gideon began climbing down the ladder.

Dalton made his way over to sit on the crates by the stalls, nodding to the bale of hay beside him. The kid moseyed over and sat on the bale of hay, using a sleeve to wipe his tears.

"You want to tell me what's going on besides a card cheat calling you and me names?" He rested his hands on his knees, waiting, wanting to give Gideon a chance to explain.

Gideon sniffled. "I'd have fought him like you said. I ain't scared. Took a lot more than the likes of him before."

He held his cane between his knees and Sable nuzzled in between them from over the stall and he nudge her away by giving her a soft shove.

"I'm from west Nebraska, but I ain't ever going back there. Never." He rubbed a sleeve across his face once more. "My real Pa died a 'fore I was born and Ma married *him* when I was small. And he never liked me on account I weren't his. He was mean to her as much as to me and one time when he hit her, I tried to stop him…"

"He put those scars on your back, boy?" He asked, though he already knew the answer.

Gideon nodded and then shrugged. "He took a crop to me more than once, but I couldn't let him hurt her... Don't know my real last name and I ain't wearing his no more, no sir. I won't. And I ain't gonna be called by the names that man in town called me either."

Now it all made sense for the most part. And the stripes on the kid's back had a bit of explanation, though it sickened him anyone would raise a whip to a child. That would also explain Gideon knowing how to do things in and around a homestead.

"Ma blamed it on account he was drunk most of the time. But I took the money she had hid, the money that was hers and I made my way on the train to leave. That's when you saw me." The boy looked at him and then down. "It was our money, not his, so it wasn't stolen, though there wasn't much."

Dawson took in a deep breath and let it out slow and sure. "You think he might be looking for you?"

"Nahh, he ain't. He'll be glad I'm gone." Gideon sulked. "But when I'm a man I'm gonna find him and give him back what he gave to her and me one stripe at a time."

"Remember boy, sometimes revenge don't taste so sweet." He gave a gentle warning of what he knew well and went on. "You got away and that's the main thing."

Gideon looked at him. "You ain't gonna report me to the sheriff, are you?"

"If I was gonna do that then I already would have. Gideon, I didn't bring you here to work as much to give you a place to be, a home if you want it and a boost at staying out of trouble. Now, I'm beholdin' to you for all the help this leg won't let me do. But Gideon, I'm not holding you here. You'll leave here because you want to not because you have to. I'm not a man whose gonna lick you when you fail, but I will expect you to behave like the young man you are." He offered the advice he held inside, unsure how anyone grew up a child but hearing his own father's voice somewhere in his own.

Gideon's chin quivered. "I wanna stay, don't mind the work none."

He tousled the boy's light hair. "Well, you've done a man's job out here already, but I'd also like you to start thinking about attending school in town. It will help to grow you up, learn you more than you think."

Gideon eyed him, his brow tightening. "Ain't no need for it, I can read and cipher like I said."

Dalton raised his brows. "I just said think on it, there's plenty more for you to learn but for now. Mrs. Holt left a stew and biscuits on the stove. What'ya, say we go see about feeding ourselves and Leona?"

"You like her don't ya?" Gideon stood to follow him shoving his hands in his trouser pockets.

He narrowed a gaze as they walked along. "It's a lot like that, boy."

"Well, she is pretty if'n she ain't dressed like a man." Gideon giggled as they walked along. "I think she likes me now on account I've been taking care of Ernest. You gonna marry her? Might not want me then."

"What? No, I mean I don't know and you ask too many questions, but regardless should a marriage come along, this is your home too." He hadn't expected that and nearly choked on his own spit.

Gideon shoved his hands into the pocket of his trousers. "Dalton. You ever gonna tell me how you hurt your leg? I mean you know about my back now."

He eyed him closer. "One of these days kid, but not now. Why don't you get Ernest out to the corral with Sable? We'll eat then then unload the shingles for the roof."

"All right, be right in." The boy ran on to Ernest leaving Dalton to think on things.

Darn kid had a lot of questions but he would tell him the truth about his leg one of these days maybe. At least he'd got Gideon talking and it seemed with both him and Leona both under his roof, the peace and quiet he'd been seeking on the homestead was anything but that. But more than worry about the homestead, it was poker that was weighing heavy on his mind. He'd sworn off the cards, but being called a coward even by Lefty Parsons hadn't settled well with him. Wylder wanted its game and he'd been thinking on that idea a bit more each day. Well, it would be best if he left the game in the past, but something was tugging him closer and closer to different decision.

Chapter Seven

The mid-day sun warmed Dalton as he rode Sable along the property lines of the homestead. Most of the property was dense forest with the clearing for the house and small barn and a wide pasture that he needed to fence at some point for Sable and eventually Ernest.

He'd spent a few hours earlier working with Gideon to make repairs to the barn and teaching the boy had been good for both of them. The kid chattered with him on and off, making the work pleasant.

He'd left the boy to look after Leona while he accomplished two things today that he'd been putting off. One was to make the purchase of women's clothing for Leona and a few new things for the boy. The other, with a bit of reluctance go ahead and tell Sonny Cash he'd sign on for a championship set of poker. It wasn't as much Lefty Parsons who had changed his mind, but it still bothered him that there were those in Wylder who hadn't forgotten the past even though little had been said. And maybe as it was, Russ Holt was right, playing might make a bit of amends for things, even if it had been out of his control how things had happened.

But he wasn't gonna loan out his name to something small. He wasn't signing on for some silly little township playoff. He would set the stakes high. If Wylder wanted his name then they needed to plan big because he wasn't doing it again.

He urged Sable onto the road toward town meeting the end of his property. The ride was nice but he couldn't keep Leona off his mind. It wouldn't be long before she'd be well enough to go back to town. Doc Sullivan had visited, but suggested a few more days of rest before she jumped back into the heavy work of washing at the dress shop.

Dalton had expected it to be a bit awkward with Leona in his bed recovering, but that had not been the case. Some part of him was reluctant that he'd be returning her to town soon.

Hell, he'd had a few special ladies, high priced whores he visited from time to time in his wanderings over the years. But he'd never held or kissed anything as lovely as Leona, and he still wasn't sure how to feel about having done so.

And now here he was, heading to town to purchase her a new wardrobe. What the hell he was doing, he wasn't sure. At first, he'd wanted to show her what a beauty she was, but now he had to admit, he'd sure like to see her wearing some of the fine things he was planning to purchase. Or better yet, peeling the items from her to discover more than he should be thinking about.

He slowed Sable at the Lowery's Dress Shoppe. His plans to purchase Leona a new wardrobe was bound to turn a few heads, as the ladies inside the dress shop were her friends. And being a gambling man, he'd bet there was no doubt this would hit the quilting circle outside the social club come Saturday.

He dismounted and tied the horse to the small hitching post and lifted his cane from the saddle. He opened the door and stepped inside the dress shop. He removed his hat listening to the flutter of ladies in conversation until he cleared his voice.

The Widow Lowery stood behind the counter, a rotund woman wearing a fancy yellow dress. "Oh, Mr. Payne, good afternoon." She fanned herself with a feathered fan. "How is Leona faring?"

"She's resting still but well." He stepped closer, leaning on his cane. So, the news was already out. "She'll be back to work here first of the week according to Doc Sullivan."

"I'm sure your acquainted with Mrs. Holt and this is Mrs. Sullivan, Doctor Sullivan's wife." The widow nodded to Laurel and the physician's wife, who were both handling a bolt of material.

He gulped a quick swallow and nodded. "Ladies." Of course, he was acquainted with Mrs. Holt who had come by the homestead to check on Leona a few times. But he'd not yet met the doctor's wife, a real beauty in her own right.

"It was certainly an awful thing those bad men who attacked poor Miss Fabray...and we'll expect her back soon then." The Widow fanned herself again, pushing her tiny spectacles up on her nose. "What brings you buy the shop today, sir?"

"Uh...I need to..." He began but noted the ladies' conversation stopped once more, both women turning to face him. "Well, I want to look at some dresses...and women's things."

The Widow lifted her brows. "Oh, my, a lady friend perhaps."

He gave a slight nod. Hell... what he expected. "Yes, uh .... a couple of your nicer gowns, hats, gloves, stockings. All the things a lady needs."

The silence of the dress shop was deafening. He forced a breath. Hell, he could handle a saloon full of men ready to take him down, but these few ladies in the dress shop might gamble him right under the nearest table.

"Yes, we have those items but may I ask would you know the woman's measurements?" The Widow waited.

"Well, she's uh..." He hesitated but what the hell now, Mrs. Holt had figured a thing or too and at this point he was already in quicksand fast. He might as well own up to it. "Actually, she's...Leona."

The Widow inquired further. "Miss Fabray's size then by comparison?"

"No Ma'am, Leona." He walked closer, keeping his voice sure.

The dress shop owners mouth dropped open.

The silence held but Mrs. Holt rushed over. "I happen to know; Leona has fancied one of the mint gowns for a long time." She sifted the wall of fancy gowns and pulled one free, holding it against her own body.

"That's a right pretty one." He focused on the light green silken garment.

"Well, I think Miss Fabray wouldn't need such a gown and this one, with some of the finest silks from back East, Mr. Payne." The Widow shook her head. "I'm afraid it's quite expensive at that, perhaps you'd care to choose from our lower priced dresses. Leona wouldn't value such an item, always in those oversized shirts and britches."

He dared to touch the satin dress. "This is more what I was looking for, though I'll take a few of the less fine gowns for her every day wear."

"I can hardly see the need for Miss Fabray to have these finer items?" The Widow all but shook her head. "Mr. Payne, where would she even wear such a immaculately made dress?"

That did it. He turned to face the woman. It wasn't often he flaunted his wealth before people but the widow had no idea what he was about to do. "Widow Lowery..." He held her gaze and stepped even closer, reaching a hand to rest on her shoulder. "I am about to spend a very great deal of money right here in your shop and I cannot think of any woman more deserving than Leona, unless of course you still find some reason to object. I'm sure there are some really nice shops as close as Cheyenne."

The other two women whispered and Mrs. Holt gave a slight giggle.

"Oh well, oh my I mean...Sir...of course. Miss Fabray with her recent attack and all is deserving of the best money can buy I suppose. Mrs. Holt will show you more of the same to Mr. Payne." She grabbed him by the arm, tugging him to one of the chairs. "And please, Mr. Payne, sit here and rest that knee of yours a bit."

The widow sat her fan aside and hurried to the counter for a pencil and tablet. "Now some of these gowns are...well around seventy to the top ones up to one hundred and fifty dollars...and would you...have a limit, sir?"

He tucked his cane between his knees. "No limit Madam. I'll want to see matching hats, scarves, boots as well as those nice...underthings woman all need." The widow's face reddened but Mrs. Holt gave him a knowing smile.

Mrs. Sullivan pulled a taffeta burnt orange dress from the far wall. "Oh, wouldn't Leona look just lovely in this one with her dark hair and her amber eyes, Laurel." She held it up for his view, modeling it over her pregnant belly.

"Oh, I do think so." Mrs. Holt responded as she pulled another, a black linen skirt and blouse with a dark feathery hat attached from the fancier choices. "And this?"

He touched the material as she walked closer, both she and Mrs. Sullivan showing him their preferences.

"Have all three wrapped up nicely, along with all the things Leona will need, and I thank you, ladies." He stood then with a nod, hoping for a quick exit once he paid. Had anything been more uncomfortable in his life?

He walked to the counter and pulled his leather wallet from his black duster and fumbled up a pile of one-hundred-dollar bills laying them on the counter. "I believe this should cover all Leona will need, Ma'am."

The Widow studied the money and sized him up. "My but this is far too much...I..."

He held up a single hand. "No ma'am I want Leona to have all she needs and you ladies treat yourselves to a very nice lunch today. I'll stop by for the packages this afternoon."

He moved toward the door but turned back. "Oh, and so as to make sure Leona can work here in her comforts how about adding a couple of those lady's pants and blouses and those brown work boots there." He pointed to the brown boots on display and put down more money.

The Widow nodded speechless and his guess was

74

that was the first time that might have ever happened.

"We'll add all Leona will need, Mr. Payne. Good day, sir." Mrs. Holt responded with a smile.

He made his way back to Sable with a chuckle, the sound of the women's voices behind him clucking like a fox had upset the hen house. What the hell of a mess he'd created now...but it seemed none would look at Leona the same again. And he suspected he'd be much the same when he saw her in those fancy dresses.

He tugged the horse to follow, heading toward the saloon. Oh, the money had been well spent and Leona was deserving of knowing what a beauty she was...and he was the one that was going to make sure of that but...

He knew better. He damn well knew better. Women could be trouble and Leona wouldn't be unique there. He had come home to retire, not to worry over the well-being of some tomboy wash woman and a kid with no home or name. Yet here he was buying Leona fine things and anticipating her wearing them—for him. Yep, he was falling and hadn't even known it himself. That one stolen kiss had done it and now there was no going back—not that he was even giving that further thought.

Dalton turned the corner and tied the horse at the hitching post outside the saloon. He grabbed his cane. With a deep breath he limped right through the double swinging doors and stopped at the bar.

The saloon showed it's age with worn curtains, a few plants and a lone piano in the corner that sounded for a few hours after dark and longer on the weekends. This would do for a big poker game. Not the chandelier halls of San Francisco or Chicago but enough for

Wylder to get what it wanted and allow him to redeem himself as a native son.

Sonny turned and held his gaze. The stand-off lasted for a moment with the oversized bar tender, but the man no doubt knew why he was here. Dalton reached into his coat pocket and lay the bills on the table spreading them out, a complete hush taking over the room.

Sonny inspected the money, summing it up. "That's....three-thousand dollars...Dalton."

He nodded. "Yep, if we're gonna host a game here in Wylder, not gonna be playing for pennies."

"All right then." The bartender laid a hand to the cash but Dalton stopped him by flattening his hand on the bills.

"I call. I'll be naming the man who holds the entry fees." His gaze landed on Russ Holt, who sat in the corner at a lone table, nursing his suds.

The older cowboy leaned back in his chair, setting his mug aside. Dalton needed a man he could count on, even until lifting his revolver if it came to it. Big games could be notorious at thieves trying to find a way to make off with the cash and he had to make sure this time.

"I'm naming Holt for the entry fees and for chaperoning of the championship." He added for all to hear. "The sheriff will have his hands full in town because we're not playing for pennies here."

"Chaperone." Sonny angled a glance at him.

"Cheating won't be tolerated. Players will be searched before each sit down. Table and chairs will be cleared. Saloon ladies will stay at the bar and not mingle among the players. Each entry pays their three grand in cash up front." He had a bit more but he'd be writing up all the rules.

Sonny exhaled an audible breath but Dalton went on. "You can serve alcohol. Open your curtains for a view. But no one lingers inside if they haven't paid to play."

Again, the silence held.

"All right then the game is on!" The saloon owner gave a reluctant nod. "You drive a hard bargain, Payne."

"That I do." Dalton laid another hundred dollars on the table. "Rounds for the house tonight."

The saloon filled again with cheers and whoops.

He angled a glance at Russ who gave him a simple nod.

"Sonny, I'll draw up a list of the rules and pay offs. I'll have Russ select a few men from town who aren't playing to observe the tables. Cheats will be tossed, no refunds. We'll fill up twenty tables and play to one winner."

"Players will be checked at each entry. Games played in full before they leave the table. Late check ins or after breaks will be terminated from the game and forfeit their winnings. Patrons can watch from outside. Entry fees will afford the town of Wylder a nice profit, and there will be more I'll outline for planning."

Sonny's brows narrowed. "Ain't many gonna afford the like but word will travel fast."

"The ones who know the game will show. Put it in the papers local, and telegraph to the bigger cities." With that Dalton lifted his cane and made his way back outside to Sable, content on finally freeing himself of the idle whispers that still accused him for the past.

****

The sun had long set across the homestead. Dalton stood at the stove salting the meat he'd just cooked in the heavy iron skillet. Gideon washed up at the sink pump as he placed beef and roasted potatoes on the table. The meat in the cast iron pot sizzled, the aroma filling the room. He hadn't yet told the kid or Leona that he'd signed on for the game but he'd set the wrapped bundles of clothing on the foot of the bed where Leona was sleeping when he'd returned. Since he'd burnt her torn clothing, she wouldn't have much choice but to wear some of what he'd purchased if she were coming out to supper.

Gideon put plates on the table. The boy knew how to help him manage meals. A lot of things about him were telling but pushing for more information shut the boy down still. He filled his cup with coffee as Gideon pumped two cups of water into tin mugs. He turned and his heart skipped a single beat.

Leona stood before them both wearing a rose-colored casual dress. She'd smoothed her hair which was brushed and placed up onto her head, revealing the light skin of her neck and the tops of her bosoms. And she was something to behold.

Gideon's mouth dropped open and he stood up straight. "Geez, Leona you look like a girl…a woman…a lady."

Dalton scanned the full length of her again. She didn't even look like the same woman, and he wasn't even sure he could form a single word, much less breathe.

"As I suspected, right beautiful." He whispered as he sat his mug of coffee on the table.

She blushed an enticing shade of pink, something rare for her. "Well, don't y'all keep a gawkin'. Ain't like I've nothing else to wear since ya' burned my clothes up."

She walked over to the table but Gideon beat her to it.

"Miss Leona allow me." The boy smiled with satisfaction as he held out her chair. "You look real fancy."

Leona's frown lessened, a grin easing across her lips. "Thank you, Gideon that's very nice like."

Dalton sat too, unable to take his eyes from her. "I hope you've your appetite back. Got some beef and roasted potatoes with carrots." He nodded for the kid to wait and offered Leona the fork first.

"I'm feeling much better, might be I can return home to work in a day or so like the Doc said." She took the fork and lifted a bit of meat to her plate, followed by a few potatoes and carrots. "This looks delicious, and I am rather famished."

Disappointment flowed through him at the thought she would return to town. He had enjoyed her company these past few days. And since that kiss they had shared...hell, he wanted more time with her. "Make sure you're ready, Doc said the leg will take some time, he don't think you should be lifting the pots yet."

"I might be a sight to see stirrin' up them pots dressed as such, but my leg's better. Everything was just sore more than anything." She leaned over her food shoveling in a bite, her elbows on the table.

Dalton found his gaze drawn to the full breasts pushed high by the bodice of her gown and the fact she wore a corset. Well, at least she was aware how to wear one. He cleared his voice and lifted his elbows, showing her as he held his fork and knife in the proper fashion for eating.

Leona mimicked him with a bit embarrassment and removed her elbows from the table. Gideon had been lookin on with keen interest and did the same once he had filled his plate.

"Wait, I think grace is called for…what'ya both say?" Dalton offered the idea though he wasn't much of a praying man himself.

She set her fork and knife down. "I reckon so, you gonna say it?"

Dalton gave it some thought. "It's been a while since I've…"

"I can do it." Gideon folded his hands and waited for Dalton's nod. "Lord, we give thanks for the bounty we are about to receive, let it nourish our bodies for thy service, Amen."

Dalton had yet to close his eyes with Gideon speaking the prayer with ease. "Thank you, boy."

"That was real nice prayer, Gideon." Leona lifted her fork and knife again, looking back at him.

Dalton took a deep breath and let it out. "I've, uh… been to town today and made the purchase of Leona's pretty new clothes and the new ones you're wearing."

Gideon glanced at his new shirt and then his boots. The boy had been speechless with several new pieces of clothing and boots much like his own.

"And I also put money down and set the rules on the poker championship for Wylder." He waited.

"You're playin'?" Gideon's voice jumped an octave as he rocked in his chair. "Holy shit."

He narrowed a hard glare on the boy. "That didn't

come from the same mouth you just prayed from, did it?"

Gideon recovered, his light hair falling across his brow. "I mean that's uh, that's great, sir."

"Boy why don't you grab a pencil and a tablet over there." Dalton suggested as he chewed a bite of the savory beef.

Gideon shoved a biscuit into his mouth and returned with the items, still chewing.

"Thought you said you're a retirin'." Leona reached for her tin of water, wrapping both hands around it and sipping.

"Well, seems the way things happened here before, this one last game might just let me redeem myself. Add these figures." He leaned to look at the tablet as Gideon wrote, not wanting to explain further, at least not until he had the right words. "We're gonna have fifteen tables of five players and the buy in is three-thousand dollars each."

"So, seventy-five playing at three-thousand dollars for each one of 'em." Gideon figured using his fingers. "That's Two-hundred and twenty five-thousand dollars." The kid whistled.

"The pot will be one-hundred twenty-five thousand, leaving Wylder how much?"

Gideon began adding things up, squinting to figure in his head

"Fifty thousand dollars for the town of Wylder and all the businesses see some profits along the way." Leona said matter-o-fact. "All a matter of luck and skill who rakes in that big sum. Seventy-five is a lot a playin'."

He studied her for the moment. "Luck's one thing

81

but skills another. Though the first few rounds will prove to lose a good number of players. Some won't last in a big game like this, losin' their money quickly."

"My Pa taught me poker a long time ago. Ain't played in a while though, but I played well a time or two." She angled a glance at him and if he were guessing with a bit of challenge in her eyes.

"I played some too." Gideon's eyes were wide with hope as he leaned on the table again.

Dalton bumped the boy's elbows from the table. "You two think it so easy, huh?" He reached into the inside pocket of his coat hanging on the back of his chair and handed a deck of cards to Gideon. "Deal 'em, boy."

"We're gonna play?" The lad fumbled to shuffle the cards several times his blue eyes bright with excitement.

"Let's see what you both have since you think it so easily done." This wouldn't last long. He reached to the counter behind him and grabbed a jar of dried beans. He divided out each of them to have twenty-five beans for betting, three small piles before him.

"Here, Dalton you cut 'em." Gideon put the mixed deck in front of him.

Dalton lifted the top half of the deck and put it beside the remainder of the cards. "There ya' go, sir."

Gideon took up the cards. "What do we play?"

"Five card draw." Leona met Dalton's gaze with a lifted brow.

"The lady spoke it." Dalton winked, still astonished at her appearance in the dress. Damn, wasn't she something to keep his sites on?

The boy dealt them five cards each and he picked

his up for a quick view. Most often, he'd wait and read the faces around him and view his cards closer to his play. He held three eights, a nine and a king.

He studied Leona. She showed nothing on her face but she did study her cards for a length of time. Was she studying a winning or losing hand? She'd looked much the same when he'd kissed her. Her cards were good then. Now he did want to chuckle. Hell, she made it hard to focus if he were being honest with himself.

He laid aside the nine and king and Gideon dealt him two more cards, a two and a six. Three of a kind with the six kicker just might take the hand.

He wasn't interested in anything more than teaching the lesson that went with betting and glad for the boy's sake it wasn't in a smoke-filled drunken saloon. "Now were we playing for money, where do we all stand?"

He pushed more beans to the center. "What would you do boy? One hundred and twenty-five thousand in your hand or no?"

Gideon looked at his cards and his face dropped with his cards. "Nahhh, I fold this hand."

"And the lady?" He couldn't resist a smile.

But Leona didn't sway. "Call, Gambler."

"Really?" He couldn't see it. "One hundred-twenty-five-thousand?"

She lifted her brows in challenge, though it was his groin that wanted to respond as he sweep her dress once more with his gaze.

"All right." He laid down his hand.

She studied his cards on the table and laid down her cards showing a full house. "Sorry Gambler. Jacks full of eights. Full house wins"

Dalton let another smile slip, pushing the pile of beans to her side of the table. "And the game goes to the lady."

"One hundred and twenty-five thousand." She laughed and clapped her hands. "Skill and luck."

"Skill," He explained, "comes with time. Boy, I knew you had nothing. And you," he held Leona's gaze. "Your eyes gave you away...they were smiling."

"But you played." She spoke. "You didn't fold, I win."

"Sure, just to show you." He offered, moving his ante to the center. "But the games not over."

"Nope, I won it against the best gambler the west has ever seen. Might be I need to sign up for that championship after all, since women can play." She folded her arms, pride crossing her face.

He held up a finger and dealt the next hand. Two hours later, he raked in the last pile of his winning beans, the boy laying his head on the table and Leona miffed at his ability to read her like a book.

"Skill comes at a price and it's any man's game at those tables and most often saloons are full of smoke and men drunk enough to shoot you. Remember that." He hinted the truth of it all.

The boy gave a nod and yawned.

"All right, Gambler, you know your poker game all right." She stood, mindful of her leg and that of straightening her dress.

He set the stack of cards aside he'd shuffled. "You played a good game, Leona, honestly a good game all along."

"Can't read you at all after a few hands. Bluffing or not." She folded her arms with a pout.

"Had a lot of years of working on it. But I think with having the game, a lot of things will be said and I need you both to listen to me. Sit. I'll clean up the dishes in a bit." He needed to tell them both the truths of the past. With the championship coming to town, rumors would fill the gossip chains and he wanted them both to hear his side of how it all happened.

"I'm gonna set things straight right here tonight, so both of you know and then I'm done with this topic, no matter what gossip you hear, you will know the truth from me." He reached for the flask inside his coat and set it on the table. The reminder brought it all back nice and clear as it did each time he sat the pint container before him or felt the weight of it in his coat.

"I was in my early twenties and good at cards and I'd traveled a bit, won some of the bigger games. Lost a lot more than I won to begin with. Winning builds a few rivals out there but I let that bottle make me a fool." He studied the flask, turning it round and round with his fingertips. "Alcohol can do that to a man."

"Whiskey?" Gideon grabbed the flask, opening and sniffing the contents with a frown.

He leaned in, taking the flask back. "A gentleman's drink, boy, bourbon."

Leona sat and leaned back in her chair angling a glance to listen, but looking at her wasn't a good idea, his thoughts lost for a moment. He gave another hard glance to the liquor.

"There was a big game here in Wylder and a lot of money in the pot. I played well and whipped my rival right out of the game but it was discovered the money in the pot was taken—missing from the bank with no explanation. So, I couldn't figure out how if he'd hadn't taken the money, where it had gone and... the woman I was to marry..."

"She took the money?" Gideons eyes widened and he stilled in his chair.

He nodded, though he waited for a reaction from Leona. "And I tried to talk her out of it, not understanding her betrayal or trusting the others accusing me. So, I shot him in self-defense, but...she got me with a bullet to the knee and ran with the money. No one even knew she had it. When it was discovered, all in Wylder thought it was me who had allowed that the happen. That I had planned that with her for the money. To meet up with her later, but that wasn't how it went and I nearly lost my leg for it."

"If I hadn't been drinking, none of it would have happened right under my nose like it did. Lots of rumors, hard feelings, lies. But I watched it hurt my father who stayed here not accepting of the bad things said about me. Didn't want him hurt, so I left and I went out there and won it all, every damn game. To prove I hadn't been that thief they called me. But rumors and lies die hard. As this game comes to town now, that will all resurface, and some will still see it the same." He leaned back into this chair, adjusting his leg to comfort.

"But you didn't do it." Gideon shook his shaggy locks.

"Nope, but I was drinking. So, I keep this bottle to remind me. I play the game, not the money. I don't cheat or allow it of others. It seems town's forgotten, but by signing on, I open all that back up for speculation. So, I've told you the truth of it. I have nothing to prove here, but if Wylder gets its game and it's money, then I settle the score somehow for my father." He wasn't sure the score would ever be settled. His knee was proof enough of that.

Leona nodded, her amber eyes solemn and as trusting as when he'd kissed her, making him lose focus on his words again. She was beautiful. He sorted his thoughts and went on. "So, I'm playing but I am wanting a buy in from you both, a trade off of sorts. If I do this, win or lose, boy, I want you to start school soon."

Gideon groaned, but nodded. "All right, I guess."

He turned to Leona once more. "And Leona you dress like a lady even when you work, even as you do each and every day. You'll be a seamstress before too long and you'll need to look like one, win the widow over on that."

She waited, keeping her poker face and then gave a pout. "All right, Gambler, but you have to take me on the picnic you promised tomorrow since it's Sunday and I gotta get back to town on Monday."

"Going to bed so I can get myself ready for school. School of all things. I already know my figures and reading…" Gideon wandered off to his room mumbling to himself as he shut the door.

Dalton put his attention back to Leona. "Does this picnic involve you wearing another of your new dresses?"

She considered, touching the fancy satin ribbon at her middle. "All right, I can wear one of the new skirts. But when I'm a workin' them hot pots I'll wear them fine ladies trouser and boots you got me, not sure I know how to work in all this fanciness."

He stood and leaned closer giving her a tender

swift kiss. She was warm and unexpecting and some part of him wasn't even sure why he did that again when he damn well knew better. "Absolutely, we'll go on a that picnic tomorrow."

Chapter Eight

A light wind bristled the trees above them as Dalton sat on a blanket beside Leona. The shade was pleasant though in the distance the sky had darkened, hinting of rain. He'd hitched Ernest to the small wagon and stopped the mule at a spot he'd found a few days back, where the grass wasn't too high and the stream had a small fall.

"I ain't about to turn down no pie, Gambler, but storms a comin' in like I told ya'. I can smell the rain, just like my Pa used to say he could." She peered into the sky, holding the small tin plate he'd handed to her.

He took a look at the distant clouds, but the view of her was worth the chance. "We're good for a bit longer."

"I suppose it's off a ways." She tasted the apple pie he'd baked early that morning. He wasn't much of a cook, but he'd learned long ago how to bake a pie from his father.

He'd thought maybe she'd become annoyed with his continuing to suggestions for her dress and manners but as it was, she hadn't. He finished his pie and set his tin plate aside and watched as she enjoyed the treat.

"What?" She touched her dress and wiped her mouth with the cloth napkin.

"Just, it's nice to see you becoming a lady, Leona." Maybe if they spent more time, he might say a lot more than that. He'd sure as hell like to when it was time. He still wasn't at all sure as to the reasons he was attracted to her when it came down to it. He supposed it was she was easy to talk to with no expectations of him or his actions, accepting him for who he was and reminding him of the man he thought he'd lost a long time ago.

"Well, you burned up my other clothes and I ain't got no more trousers 'ceptin the new ones, Gambler. Not like you gave me much choice about it." She sipped her lemonade and then set her mug aside.

"It's becoming." He sipped his own tin of the refreshing tart drink.

"Becoming what?" She wiped her mouth with the cloth napkin adding it to the plate once more.

He chuckled and shook his head. "It's becoming...watching you discover how really beautiful you are, though I think you still have no idea."

"My Pa always said I's a lot like my Ma I guess." She shrugged.

"What did your father do?" He asked, curious if nothing else.

"Farming, selling his produce and trading a few furs when he trapped in the winters. We didn't have much, but I think when I was a young 'un I didn't know that. He was good to me after Mama was gone, always made sure I went to school. Though it was the boys there that made fun of me in my pants, and worse funnin' me when I did wear a dress. Made me cry and run home and I never much wore another dress cause of that. At least till now. But you make me feel real pretty, Gambler." She smiled, a slight blush crossing her cheeks. "Beautiful...even."

He set their drinks on the small crate to the side of

the blanket and moved closer to her, interested in her stories of how she grew up. Listening to her voice was calming in a way.

"He always promised he'd take me to the ocean one day, but I suppose the time just never came for us to do that, just weren't much money for travel or fine clothes like this." Her voice faded as she stared off into the distant storm.

"Leona, you are made for those things if you believe you are." He brushed back a strand of her dark hair.

She held his gaze with those amber eyes. "I've been saving my money, though I first bought Ernest and one day I'll have enough to go all the way to the ocean and stay as long as I want."

He studied her lips, full and plump, her skin smooth and flawless. Damn, but she'd missed the point he could make it all happen with ease. "Leona, one day I'm gonna take you to see that big damn ocean with all it's blue."

She narrowed her gaze, and whispered. "You're a starin' at me like ya' did when you kissed me, Gambler. You about to do that again?"

He found her abrupt. "Would you want me to?"

She sipped lemonade and set the glass back on the crate. "I liked it all right, but it made my lips tingle and…" She went on, her cheeks flushing pink. "Did you like it…when you did it to me, cause I ain't ever been kissed a 'fore you?"

"I liked it very much." He leaned in taking a small kiss across her tender lips and then nipped a second. "You smell like that lilac perfume Laurel brought to you."

"You want me to open up my mouth, Gambler?" She left her lips partially open.

Well, she could change the mood real fast. He held up a finger and smiled anyway. "Not supposed to ask. Let me show you what I mean. Lay back."

"You ain't gonna try to poke me are you, Gambler?" Her mouth dropped open.

He fell to his back beside her, defeated. This woman was gonna take a lot of fine tuning. He turned to his side resting a hand on her flat belly. "No, Leona. Not unless you want me to, but one step at a time. Lay back. Gonna kiss you for now is all."

He eased her back on the blanket and tossed his hat aside. He held her gaze for a long moment, waiting. "Close your eyes and how about I take the lead here."

Her lids slammed shut and she lay still.

Leaning, he placed his lips to hers, tentative, teasing and tasting. She opened her lips accepting his urging. She tasted of the sweetness of the lemon drink and his groin tightened.

He continued, touching her tongue with his own and letting his hand massage under her breast and then along her hip. He moved his lips to her cheeks and her chin and then her ears, her breath coming hard as he whispered. "See...it's all about letting it happen, not talking about it. How did that feel?"

She smacked her lips, tasting. "Wet and lemony."

He lifted her chin to his lips once more applying a single kiss. "What did your body feel. Leona? Because mine felt a hell of a lot more than that."

She frowned knitting her brows together, her face still close to his. "Tingles all over, and I can't even breathe, Gambler."

"That's how you are supposed to feel." he whispered.

"Do you.... mean..." She pressed her lips tight stopping again.

He nodded, urging her, his hand underneath her breast again. "Tell me…"

"I felt it...making my breath all short like I said." She held his gaze, her cheeks flushed red. "And I felt it where maybe I shouldn't have…. Gambler. Like maybe I wouldn't mind so much being poked."

"That's what I mean, but it's not poking, Leona, or at least it won't be when you and I do it. But even kissing and holding hands can be nice. And besides, you're a lady and the term poking is for whores or the like." He scooted closer to her, "One kiss at a time for the moment, because you are special, not quick fun, but something I'd like to have when the time is right for us."

"My mama told me never lay with a man. But when you kiss me Gambler, I ain't paying much attention to my Mama's words and I want you to touch me...everywhere." She dropped her gaze but then looked at him again.

He gave up and fell to his back on the blanket beside her, tugging her to lay next to him "Leona, you might be asking for more than you want right now, girl."

"Well, Laurel told me it's a nice thing sometimes and Sarah too but all I seen of those no goods at the saloon is ruttin' in the alleys." She said it as if it was normal. "Or animals…"

He rolled to her side, covering her mouth with his hand. Damn, he was gonna have to start from scratch with this woman. "We are people, not animals, Leona...let's leave that picture out of this conversation, cause when I get to love you, it's gonna be way more than what you've seen, I promise."

She gripped his hand, studying their entwined fingers.

"Look, with a man and a woman there's desire and wanting to touch, talk like we are now. Kissing like we just did and letting those feelings tangle around the pleasures of each other." He explained as best he could, wanting to be so deep inside her he wasn't sure of his own damn desires. "But make no doubt, I want you...so damn much, it's hard to hold myself back."

He raised himself over her and took her mouth, teasing his way inside her and doing so until she began to kiss him back. Damn, he did want her...so much so if she'd been a knowing woman, he'd take her now. But she was special and deserved a bit of what he was doing in teaching her first.

He eased his palm under her breast and moved his mouth to her cheeks and then her neck. She sighed, bringing him a smile of satisfaction.

"My heart is beating so fast." She touched his beard, tentative at first. "So soft. Gambler?"

"Huh?" He kissed her neck again, tasting the salt of her smooth skin, nipping and teasing with his tongue.

"I think I feel that desire of yours against my leg right now." She placed a hand to her mouth and giggled.

"Well then, you'll know how much I am feeling you in places too." He chuckled.

Rain began falling in sprinkles. He kissed her anyway with the most passion he could, searing and tasting her lips.

"Gambler?" She questioned again her fingers twisted into his hair

"Huh."

"It's a rainin' like I said." She giggled, her chest panting. "But I don't want you to stop."

"That it is, but I'm not done here yet." He placed his lips to hers and took her mouth in another heated kiss. "Let the rain come, girl. Let's head back."

"Dalton…" Leona's heart raced as she and the Gambler raced back to his homestead in the pouring rain. The downpour had tugged them apart and he'd tossed her in the wagon and urged Ernest to a fast jaunt back. He'd turned the mule into the small corral after unhitching him from the wagon, telling her to run on inside.

She entered, the light of a single lamp on the table giving the home a soft glow. She used a cloth to dry her hair. The pitter of rain along the roof quickened as the door opened and Dalton entered, shaking his hat off and setting it aside as he focused on her.

In that moment it became clear to her that his kisses had fevered them both, past the point of wanting something she wasn't even sure she understood. He made no haste in pulling her into his arms kissing her again. He sure had a passion for kissing and the depths of her would allow him anything…anything at all.

"I'm thinking that right time you mentioned might be now." She said it a bit frightened at how intense her body was responding to him. And as if she couldn't help it, she clung to him, deepening the kiss. She opened her mouth as they swayed together, his breath heavy. He tugged on her bottom lip and held her back from him.

"Leona, I want to do right by you, not take advantage but…damn it's been a long time for me." His voice was a deep whisper of urgency.

She sucked in a swift breath, so needy for his touch she shivered. "I ain't some young girl anymore… and if any man's ever a gonna make me a woman, it should be you who shows me."

He smoothed her hair, placing his hands to her blouse, easing each button loose as his deep green eyes held her hostage. He glanced to the second room where Gideon slept as he eased them into the room with his big bed and shut the door.

"Leona, tell me to stop…tell me and I will." He waltzed her closer to the bed, in spite of his words, his warm lips on her neck and shoulders as he drew her blouse away. It fell to the floor. How had he done that so easily?

He brushed a palm across her nipples pushed high by her stays and she shivered, sucking in a swift breath as the sensation.

He drew her to him with the open-mouthed kisses she craved. She obliged, a moan slipping as he loosened her stays and lifted the garment from her with a practiced ease. Naked. Her breasts were bared to him, though she wanted to cover herself. He bent his head and his warm mouth covered a nipple.

She gasped as he licked and drew on her with effort. She flushed the full length of her body as if heat had come from her own depths. Was this what men desired, to taste breasts and skin? Oh, what was she to do with her whole body wanting more of what…? She ran her hands into the length of his hair holding him to her.

"Gambler..." she whispered, urgent, when he teased her other nipple, his hand cupping her breast to lift it to him, she bit her bottom lip to avoid the sigh of pleasure that wanted to escape her.

Her hands continued to play in his hair as he worked from one breast to the other. It was pleasant, drawing a warmth between her thighs where he'd yet to touch her. He was so tall, he had to bend, yet she leaned back, wanting his warm mouth to keep at it.

"Shouldn't we go.... the bed?" She whispered, but he sat in the chair and as he did, her skirt and pantaloons left her, pooling to the floor. He'd done that without her having an inkling. Now she was fully naked before him, yet she didn't shy. She kicked from her boots and struggled out of her stockings.

Heat flushed her cheeks and upper body as he took the full view of her, looking his fill. The small lamp lit the room a hint of gold. She'd never been shy in the least, but this was different, as if she wanted him to see her without her clothes. As if she wanted him to have all of her open to him. Was that so wrong given how she was feeling?

"You are so damn beautiful, Leona. It's all right." His whisper was heavy as he removed his shirt, letting it drop. He stepped from his boots, the heavy thud of each echoing as they hit the floor. His muscles were thick and his chest covered with a scattering of dark hair. His words eased her as touched her there.... there where no man had ever been.

Her lips parted and she shivered when his fingers parted her, searching and teasing. A soft moan left him as he found her. She grabbed onto his shoulder to keep her balance. So personal, but her breath held short as he played there on the center of her so gently. She craved more of what she wasn't sure. She fought to move with him, so sensitive, so tender until the stretch of his fingers pressed inside her. She tensed, unsure of what he was doing, and pushing away.

"Easy, girl." He whispered as he worked further, keeping her against him.

Laurel had told her more of what a man's touch could bring and she thought she understood, though she'd said it took a bit of time to learn each other. Well, she was a learning fast right now as his thick fingers stretched her. He pushed her legs apart as she held onto him. He explored her with his fingers so gentle it was shocking. "Gambler should we.... the bed."

He answered in a soft growl. "Not yet."

And then his fingers pressed fully inside her, so deep she sucked in a hard breath, uncertain.

"It's all right, not gonna hurt you." His whisper eased her but she clenched tight as he moved his fingers and clamped his mouth on a nipple. She wanted to shriek but bit her bottom lip to allow it. It was a tortuous thing his fingers inside her and a thumb against her pleasure as his mouth worked across yet the other nipple.

"Dalton...please…" She began to rock, reaching for more of what he was doing. Her body rose as she begged again, her legs quivering with each stroke across the bud of her pleasure. He had to stop but she wanted...something and he pinned her to him, increasing the work of his fingers.

"Let go, Leona…" He gave a gravelly whisper and drew hard on a nipple.

And then it came fast as she bowed, crossing over to the swift bolts of pleasure that his fingers touched deep inside her. And the breathy cries were her own as he held her, not letting her fall away from him. He worked his fingers to see her through and she cried out at the blissful heat coursing through her center again and again.

Her chest pounded and her breath was short, but she floated back to him. She closed her eyes as he removed his fingers, aware he was settling her to straddle him across the chair. He was a large man, his trousers pushed below his hip revealing all of him to her. She blinked hard and gulped as he eased her legs wider. And the pain she'd expected found her as he pulled her down without mercy, filling her with a heavy growl that mingled with her screech of pain.

"Shhhh." His cheek was against hers. "No way to do that easy...it'll lessen. Let me have you Leona…"

Leona bit her bottom lip, not having known this was another way of doing things with him in a chair. And it hurt, making it difficult to breathe.

"Gambler..." She tried to protest, but he eased her up and back down. She grimaced at the shearing stretch he caused again and again as he moved her on him, slow and steady.

"It's all right..." His hand eased between them touching the sensitive pearl of her, teasing once more. She tried to relax, but how could she? It hurt and was pleasant at the same time.

He moaned, his deep green eyes holding her as he increased the pace of his fingers. She moaned at the warmth building there inside her once more, the pain and pleasure mingling to take her breath. How did he know this about her body, things she didn't even know...?

He eased his hands to her hips and behind to her bottom pulling her onto him as he thrust harder. He rubbed her backside, his mouth along her breasts feasting, his breath hard on her skin. It was going to happen again and she wasn't sure with the pain if she could...

She bit her bottom lip. "Oh...Gambler..."

"I'm hurting you?" He asked, though he never stopped the motion.

She fought to find her words. "No...oh...it wants to happen again...oh, please..."

He grabbed her by the hips, pounding her to him. All she could do was hang onto him, stretching to open herself for him. She tried to hold back but he brought her down faster and faster. She bowed away from him and cried at the searing bliss that consumed her where he filled her. Her breath lost to cries that ran out of air.... yet she clung to him still.

And then it faded, her heart pounding hard inside her chest, leaving her spent to fall against him. He kissed her and held her close calling her name as his own body shuddered hard as his kisses seared her neck.

He brushed her hair back from her face to kiss her. Then he lifted her and lay her in his big bed. He lay down beside her and drew her close, covering them both with the quilt. "Never held anything so sweet as you Leona, it'll be better next time."

She turned to him then. "Gambler, I think I'm a gonna love you for a long, long time if'n that's all right."

He tugged her against him, his breath still hard.

"It's perfectly all right, Leona…for a long, long time."

Chapter Nine

Dalton carried the bag of Leona's things from the small wagon to the door of her room in the back of Lowery's Dress Shoppe. She was ready to be back to work even if she complained of the widow's demands most of the time. But the old woman had welcomed her back with a bit of fuss that she take it easy for several more days.

She had been chatty the entire ride but hadn't mentioned the night before. He'd hinted but she hadn't commented further though a pleasant blush had crossed her cheeks as well as a smile.

He had to admit he was reluctant to bring her back to town and no longer have her in his bed. That damn big mattress of his would be lonesome without her for sure now. And what the hell had he done in making love to her anyway? He'd never be the same man again it seemed. He was ready for what touching her like that might mean for their future. Somehow, marriage didn't seem so far from what his life needed. Well, he'd have to work on making that happen.

"I reckon I'm back and time to get to my work." She set the bag on the small wooden bed. Her room was small but tidy, with a dresser and a tiny mirror on a stand.

"You take it easy in the heat like the doc said." He leaned on his cane, his leg paying the price for his efforts in loving her last night.

"I... thank you for the care and..." That enticing pink shaded her face once more.

He winked. "I won't be far..."

"Gambler?"

He looked at her.

"Last night was.... well, it was.... I best get to my work." On a hop she'd plopped a kiss to his cheek and made out the door.

Hell, he wouldn't be a long way's off but he should use more discretion. Rumors could fall into unneeded places and were she to be with child.... well, that would be unfortunate at this time, though he wouldn't say so if they were married. But for now, there was much he needed to get to before he could even wrap his thoughts around making Leona his wife.

He'd dropped Gideon off at the mercantile with a few dollars to purchase a slate and chalk, a tablet and pencils that he'd need for school. While he had the kid willing to go, he wasn't going to delay things in getting him started beginning today.

He left Ernest outside the back of the dress shop and walked on foot toward the mercantile to meet Gideon. As he got closer the boy ambled down the stairs carrying a slate and books. He was a handsome boy with his light hair combed and new clothing including a ribbon tie. With any luck he'd stay in school with the promise of a horse all his own.

"You find all you needed, boy?" He asked as they walked toward the school.

"Mr. Wylder got it together, let me know what all the other kids take with them, but I still don't want to go." Gideon shrugged and then shrugged with a pout.

"No backing out now, I'm playin' the game and you're going to school." He rested a hand on Gideon's shoulders as they walked, the school appearing in the distance.

"But you ain't even played a game yet and..." Gideon stopped mid-sentence.

"School is part of the deal." Dalton nodded toward the schoolhouse where children played outside.

"But I ain't gonna know nobody or the teacher. And besides you need me to help you cause of your knee." The boy gave his best efforts.

"I'll be fine." He handed the kid a lunch pail he'd packed with two sandwiches and an apple. "See you this afternoon. I've got business in town anyway."

Gideon took his lunch and scratched at his collar. The boy fidgeted, glancing at the other children.

He could understand the apprehension. "Look, you stay in school for a month, and I'll get you that horse I promised. You drop out of school, and I'll sell him out from under you as is fair."

"Never had my own horse." The boy's eyes widened.

He nodded. "Go on then."

The boy took a deep breath and glanced at the school and back to him and went up the steps and inside..

Dalton hesitated but then followed as more children inside the school himself. He waited in the back as the students took their seats in a scuffling rush.

Miss Bloom, the teacher, had dark hair held in a chignon and violet eyes, pretty in her own rights.

"Children. Take your seats. Quiet now." She sifted through papers but lifted her gaze as Gideon approached her desk. "Hello. And you are?"

He fumbled with the hat in his hands. "Gideon, Ma'am."

"Oh, well welcome to school." She smiled and sat to write his name in her ledger. "And your family name?"

The boy dropped his gaze to snickers from the other children.

"Payne." Dalton stepped up, holding his hat in his hands.

The boy he now called son looked at him and then turned back to the teacher. "Gideon Payne, Ma'am."

"All right then, Gideon, you can have a seat there on the second row." Miss Bloom pointed and he made his way to take a seat.

Dalton placed the hat back on his head and eased from the school room, leaving the boy to it.

He crossed the street and made his way toward the saloon. The town bustled with activity with the upcoming big poker championship. He nodded to the men outside and entered through the double swinging doors.

"Tables are fillin' up, Dalton." Sonny grabbed his attention standing on a ladder at the large chalking board that had arrived from San Francisco.

He'd been keeping a check on the listing, and tipped his hat at the man. "It's coming together then."

"Yes, sir, about to fill this board up, biggest game the township has ever seen." The saloon owner jumped down. "Thirsty, Payne?"

"Coffee." He eyed Russ Holt sitting in the corner at a lone table. He made his way over; setting is hat aside. He took one of the chairs with the older man's nod to it.

"That's lists grows a bit day by day there." Holt nodded at the board and drank down his beer holding it up for another.

"That's the idea." He stretched his leg out and settled his cane aside.

"You were looking close at those names there." Russ leaned back in his chair his long gray hair falling across his brow, his thick mustached covered in suds.

"Just checking out the competition." He studied the board further.

"Each man and woman have a story up there, including you." Holt narrowed a gaze on him, handing off his empty glass as Sonny placed a new one before him.

"My story's written." He waited on Sonny to set a mug of black coffee down. "This game belongs to the town."

"You bet it does." The bartender chuckled and wandered away once more.

Russ gulped from his mug and wiped a sleeve across his moustache. "Towns not looking back much, Dalton. No one's keeping score 'cept you."

Russ Holt was a wise man, though he hadn't ever been sure about the demons that drove the old man to drink. "Not keeping score, just hoping this last one lets me retire as planned."

Russ leaned closer. "You playin' to win or just playin'?"

He took a gulp of the coffee. "I've a better question. Why's your name not up there?"

Holt's brows lifted as did a smirk. "Cause you asked me to be security. Besides, never could beat the likes of you. So, we got any trouble on that list there?"

He'd played the tables with Russ and his late brother Richard Holt, but neither had ever bested him. He took a look at the board again. "Lefty Parsons. Cheats from way back. Always a little something new and untried. Took his money last year in Reno and he's not very forgiving."

"Uh huh." Russ ogled the board again. "And what about Locke and all his sidewinders? They've been throwing money around like candy all week."

"He plays hard. Never known him to cheat." He'd played with the man enough to be certain. "Steel markets dropped. Might want to win bad enough to try."

"And Alice O'Hare…" Russ smirked with a shake of his head.

"One fine lady who knows the game. Comes from money and don't care if she losses it." He and Alice went way back, but that was as much as he'd share there.

Russ chuckled, leaning on the table and lowering his voice. "She rolled in town off the stage from Denver yesterday all feathers and little dress with a gaggle of women just like her. Took up residence in one of the boarding houses, insisting on all the rooms."

"She's clever, but she won't cheat. Too much pride." Damn, he hadn't known Alice had arrived. He figured she'd show, but he'd have keep his distance from her while he was wandering around town.

"What about Gordon Conroy?" Russ took a gulp of his beer. "Rode in here alone this morning. Slapped his money on the table without so much as a word, signing his name."

He glanced at the board again. "Most often sends a

man ahead of him to place his money down." Conroy had been here back in the day, and he couldn't be sure the bastard was worth trusting.

Russ shuffled in his chair. "Seems I remember him being here before, wearing a temper."

"Never known him to cheat but he's a right angry sore loser." He shook his head and sipped the hot coffee. "Make sure you take his weapons; he'll shoot a cheat right at the table." He'd seen that happen a couple of times in the past.

"Ain't no weapons crossing those double doors," Russ tossed a thumb over his shoulder. "But the drink will cause friction. Got Caleb, Daniel and Callum inside with me. Course the sheriff's got his hands full in town."

Dalton sat back in his chair and lifted the mug of coffee again. There would be those that would cheat or try, others who left with losses, but the most danger always seemed to be when the last few tables played. Caleb, Daniel and Callum were local ranchers and all were trustworthy if Russ has pulled them in.

"What about the Mexican there and the Indian for that matter?" Holt asked chugging his brew to empty another.

He eyed the board. Javier Gonzales was a rich rancher from Mexico, enjoyed the game for what it was, and John Littlefoot was a half-breed Sioux out of the Dakotas, a man who had never claimed to be an Indian, spending his rich white father's money. "Gonzales plays fair. Littlefoot too, though both may need a hand if it gets rowdy. Some don't like it much we allow all who can pay to play. Them and Alice anyway, a little lookout they aren't harassed, her being a woman and all."

"We'll keep shop." Russ lifted his mug. "Hey, Sonny? Another."

Dalton looked at the empty mug. "And what about you?"

"What about me?" Russ folded his arms.

"Time to start backing off the drink." He held his voice steady in warning.

The bartender came around the counter and set another glass before Russ.

The older cowboy pushed it aside. "All right.".

"Dalton? Need a refill?" Sonny asked.

"Nahh. I'm good."

"Well, a couple more names and you'll have enough players. Games can start." Russ added. "Might wanna ease yourself over to the social club for a little relaxin'."

He let a grin slip. "I'll leave that one to you, Sir. Miss Addie runs a tight ship, best to keep it that way."

"You ain't dippin' it there...makes me wonder if that has anything to do with that feisty wash woman mending at your place." Russ didn't say anything more but it was clear he was waiting on an answer.

Dalton held his poker face and the man's gaze.

"As I suspected." Russ cackled. "Saw the sheriff sending those two who attacked her off with Federal Marshal. She healed or you healing her a bit?"

He glanced around them not surprised at the interrogation. "She's much better, brought her back to town earlier."

"Oh, your secret's safe here. She's a right pretty woman, though I reckon she don't much know it. 'Bout time someone took notice of her." Russ leaned back in his chair.

"Ain't much in the way of secrets but interested in protecting her reputation." Dalton wasn't as worried about Russ as he might be those around town looking for a bit of gossip. "She was at my place recovering long enough for people to talk, but I suppose they'll talk anyway."

Russ went on. "Caleb's wife Laurel speaks highly of her. She spends a good deal of time at the ranch, good with that boy of theirs. About time she was treated well by someone."

"I aim to do just that." He turned the mug of coffee with both hands. It was awkward but there was no reason for secrets, given his newly discovered feelings for Leona.

Russ studied him for a long moment. "You been a ramblin' man for a long time to settle down with a woman, that one as feisty as you'll find I'm sure."

"Just minding my fences for now."

"What about the boy?" Russ eyed the glass before him, though he didn't pick it up.

"What are you, part of the town quiltin' circle?" Dalton sucked in a deep breath. "Didn't plan on him either but he's been a big help if I can keep him out of trouble and in school."

"You're a good man, Dalton. Known that for a long time." Russ tapped a fist on the table. "Caleb said you'd asked about a horse for the boy, is all."

"I promised if he stays in school. I'll make the purchase in a month or so." Dalton leaned up to stretch his back. "He's a good boy, came from a bad situation."

A young fancily dressed man pushed through the double swinging doors. "Names Leo Castle, finest poker professional around. Where do I toss my money this fine afternoon, gentleman?"

Dalton lifted his gaze as did Russ to the young man waving his money around in his fist. He stood tall and lanky, and strapped around his hips were silver double revolvers.

Sonny slapped a paper down before the young man. "You pay to play right here. Read the rules first then sign, kid."

"Ain't no kid, right nineteen years old as of today, a full-grown man. But when I rake in the winnings, you can call me anything you like." Castle studied the large chalk board. "Boy, names like Parsons and Locke, Gonzales....and damn, Dalton Payne."

"Sitting right there." Sonny sent a thumb over his shoulder toward Dalton.

"If it isn't indeed. What a pleasure, sir." Castle tipped his hat and smiled.

Dalton nodded, having seen the like before. But players would show up from all over and for a lot of different reasons.

"Boys, names Leo Castle. Gonna bring this win home to big sky Montana. Kid Castle they call me." The young man gave a salute and cheers erupted inside the saloon.

"And some things never change." Russ pushed the beer further from him.

Dalton nodded in agreement.

****

Morning had come early across the town of Wylder, the sun creating fractures of light between houses and buildings. Leona lifted a match and struck it across wooden table edge. The table behind her was piled high with wash, designating it a busy day for sure.

She was tired from her recent recovery but there was nothing to do but to jump in and get it all caught up. It was good to be back, but the work seemed a bit harder with her leg stiff and her back sore.

She grabbed the last bucket of water and added it to the furthest pot, thinking of Dalton. He stayed in her thoughts and somehow, she couldn't keep from smiling. She was a woman now, his woman and there were times she was sure she needed to pinch herself that it was all real.

Mary set up the ironing board on the outside back porch of the dress shop and smiled at her. Well, it would be better if she said nothing about Dalton to any of the woman at the dress shop, except of course, Laurel.

She'd scolded herself some over the fact she should have never gotten naked with Dalton Payne, but she'd been powerless in her need of him. Not that she understood how her body had melted to his touch at all. She had known better but when he'd kissed her and touched her, it had been so easy to let him touch more and more of her.

Not once had she even seen a grown man naked at least not up so close, till him. It had hurt at first, letting him poke her, though he liked to call it making love. It had been so intense she was sure she might have even passed out for a time when the pleasure had found her. But he'd been a bit worried of talk that might happen, given she could become pregnant if they kept things up.

The third pot began to collect bubbles around the base. She grabbed the closest pile of clothing. Little by little she fed all the items into the heated water adding soap and stirring the heap. Some said Ms. Jamison at the apothecary had herbs that didn't let a baby be made. But stopping by there would surely turn a few heads and start gossip.

Oh, how could that matter given she was as giddy as a school girl in love. She couldn't even sleep. She couldn't eat either. And, all she thought about all day besides these darn pots was Dalton. She'd gotten use to his tender, deep voice and his touch when he'd cared for her. He was a good man and she had no doubts of that. Some folks in town thought well of him and she hadn't heard the negative comments he was sure would surface. And now he was gonna play that big poker game. Wouldn't the town of Wylder be happy about that? Maybe they'd even forget the past like he hoped.

Funny, Dalton had more money than she'd ever even dreamed about, yet besides buying her these nice clothes he hadn't been showy about it. He sure did dress fine enough, reason for her to think she might wear some of them fancier dresses one day. Not that she would like it much. She missed the comfort of her sloppy, big clothes. Right now her lady's britches and button shirt he'd bought her were a bit itchy and tight.

She peered behind her where the widow stood inside the dress shop watching her. The old, grouchy woman had been a bit nicer to her and had even suggested she take on some of the mending. With Laurel expecting again, the widow was going to need her and had figured that she supposed.

She wiggled her toes inside her new brown boots. They were quite comfortable, unlike the clothing. She was dressed too nice for the hot pots before her, but she'd noticed a few men taking second looks at her.

And while she wasn't admitting much about liking her new work clothing, maybe she did want to prove to this town she was anything but the simple woman most thought her. And part of her love for Dalton was based on the fact he'd figured that out all by himself. Maybe he did love her as he said and even if she was afraid the fall might come, she was hanging on as tight as she could for now. Wasn't that what a woman in love did? With a contented smile, she returned to stirring the pots once more.

****

Dalton froze in his tracks, scanning town for a quick escape. Before him, Alice O'Hare and entourage of fancily dressed women came up the way, right toward him. He turned to look behind him. Nowhere to go. He should have known to avoid town mid-day given the number of people roaming the streets.

Alice sashayed toward him, the ladies following. "Well, if it isn't the gold mine himself."

Too late, she'd spotted him. Now would be a good time for the earth to open and swallow him whole. "Hello Alice, you're looking as lovely as ever—"

He'd no sooner spoke the expected niceties when she ran smack into him, leaving the following of fine ladies to plant a wet sloppy kiss right on his mouth.

Her flowery perfume invaded his senses as he fought to detach her, about the same time Leona turned the corner. Her eyes widened and her mouth dropped open and she narrowed her gaze and turned away.

He wrestled Alice aside, turning toward the dress shop. "Leona? Wait."

Damn, he'd pay hell explaining this one. Of all the luck. "Leona...wait. Sorry Alice, see you at the

114

tables...."

He brushed the back of his hand across his mouth still fighting to rid himself of Alice.

"Come to the boarding house later on Dalton and I'll make your night..." She laughed and let go of him though she blocked his way.

"Awe, I just bet you could, Alice, but...we both know that's not a good idea. I'm nothing but trouble." He pushed past her, though some of the other ladies now blocked his view of where Leona had gone.

"Hold on a minute." She glanced across the way to where Leona was at her wash once more. "What's that look Dalton Payne? You and that silly wash girl...of all the....?" She didn't finish but instead laughed.

The last thing he needed was Alice O'Hare causing trouble. "I gotta go, Alice. Ladies…"

He tipped his hat and made his way toward Leona. This wasn't going to be easy. He waited for a passing wagon and removed his hat as he approached her at one of the pots.

She stirred the pot before her with a large wooden paddle. No matter what he said, she wouldn't understand there was nothing between him and Alice and never had been. Oh, Alice would prefer it different but he'd never had a passion for the big bosomed blond.

"You needn't come along here no more, Gambler." She leaned into the spatula, stirring with more effort. Mary set her iron aside and retreated inside the dress shop, leaving them alone.

"Leona what you saw there...that's just Alice. She's...overly social about things.... hugs and kisses all the men, plays her part well with all the flaunting and flirting." He stepped closer fumbling with his hat. Hell, he had no interest in the soul sucking woman and never had.

"Seen what I seen, Dalton." Her voice was tight, her brows narrowed as she continued to stir, not so much as looking at him.

"Leona, Alice is just like that and we go way back but there has never been anything now or in the past for us." He eased a bit closer, almost gritting his teeth at how much he despised the woman.

She cut him off. "Back where.... her bed. It's all right, Gambler, maybe I knew this was gonna happen all along." She grabbed a pile of clothing and dumped them into the steaming water. "Should 'a known you were like all the rest, just funning me all along."

He followed, shaking his head. "No, that's not what I am doing. I'm trying to explain."

She went back to the first pot, and stirred again. "Ain't nobody's fool Gambler, least not until now."

No, he wasn't going to let her think what she was about this. He grabbed her by the arm and turned her. "Leona...look..."

"I done seen enough." She folded her arms but not before he noticed the tears.

He took her hand and though she resisted, he held it tighter. "Leona. I didn't kiss her, she grabbed me. It isn't what you think...it isn't."

"It sure is.... you got lip paint all on you face." She brushed away tears. "Best you get on outta here 'afore the Widow gets her broom after ya. I good mind to call her."

He followed, slapping the hat on his head and turning her once more. "Leona, the only woman who has managed to turn my head in the last ten years is you...only you. And furthermore, I have never loved any woman as much as I love you. I've never even told a woman I loved her...not until you."

Her big amber eyes held him at the same time the back door to the dress shop opened. The widow and other ladies from the dress all stood there, gawking. Well, wasn't this a fine fix. Maybe the new found audience would be of some help. "Ladies… I'm sorry to interrupt your afternoon." He touched the brim of his hat with a nod.

She glanced at her friends and back to him, folding her arms.

"All, right then." Well, what did he have to lose now? "Ladies, I'm trying very hard to convince this woman of my love and so if you'll all excuse us, we'd like a bit of privacy."

The widow's mouth fell open. Sarah tugged Mary from view and Laurel shut the door behind them all.

"Now, Leona, I will meet you right here after your work is done and I am taking you to a nice supper at the hotel like it or not. It's the least I can do for upsetting you even though my intentions were innocent." He pulled her to him. "I love you…only you."

Leona's frown tilted into a bit of a smile. "All, right, but you done it now."

"How so?"

"Widow will be at the sewing circle outside the Wylder County Social Club this Saturday and they'll all know what you just said, 'bout loving me." She angled a glance, hands on her hips. "And they're a gonna know you took me to a fine meal too."

He glanced back at the door where the woman still peeked through the small window. Well, nothing like the present to set things straight. "All right, then let's give them something the talk about." With that he drew her to him and placed his lips to hers and kissed her until she moaned and drew back.

"Gambler, if you're a funnin' me again..." The pout she held turned to a grin.

"Woman, I'm not funning at any of this, not ever...wouldn't even lie to that darn quilting circle to keep my love a secret." He smiled as she gave in and stepped into his embrace giving his heart a smile.

Chapter Ten

Darkness filled the skies west of Wylder as the sun drifted below the earth. Dalton walked from the saloon out to the streets, making his way across town. He'd left Sable at the livery and spent all evening in the saloon chatting with Russ Holt and Sonny Cash, planning for the big game. There were numbers of things to plan out. He'd left Gideon at the homestead, letting him know it might be late before he arrived home, but that wouldn't be the entire truth of things. He held back a grin.

It had been several days since he'd taken Leona to that nice dinner at the hotel and after watching her all evening in one of the fancier dresses, he had assured her it wouldn't be long before he made his way to her one night. The comment had left her wearing a hint of a pink cheeked smile. At least as it was, she'd forgiven him of the mishap with Alice O'Hare.

Lowery's Dress Shoppe sat in the darkness. Lights from other buildings cast it in shadows. He eased past the entrance and waited as a couple strolled past and then stepped to Leona's door on the back side of the building. He turned the doorknob and it clicked open. He slipped inside closing the door behind him as he let his eyes adjust to the small flame on a candle on the table. He turned and then gulped for a single breath he wasn't sure he could take.

Before him, Leona stood in her night dress, her

dark hair hanging down on one shoulder. Even in the darkness of her room, there was no way to miss the beauty of her.

"Took you a long enough, Gambler. About to come outta my skin a waitin'." She folded her arms, the small candle tossing light through the sheer material, leaving him to suspect that was all she might be wearing. Well, if that brought his trousers to life.

"Damn, Leona...aren't you a real beauty." He placed his hat on the table and lowered his gun belt, hanging it over the back of one of the small chairs.

"Like what you see Gambler?" She stepped closer and curtsied to show her gown. "It's right pretty and so soft. I ain't a wearin' no drawers neither, makin' it easier to get to things."

He grinned and tugged her to him, wrapping his arms around her. He kissed the top of her head, the smell of Lilac consuming him. "Waited all day to hug you for a moment first, girl. Not gonna rush a second of this."

"I missed you, too." She leaned up to kiss him, ravaging his mouth in an open-mouthed kiss, running her hands over his clothes. "I want you to make me have the pleasure again, Dalton, over and over."

Dalton pulled her back. "Slow down, Leona, hurrying just means it ends sooner."

"I can't help it." She was breathless, still clinging to him. "All I can think about is you touching me again like ya' did. We gotta be quiet with the widow a sleepin' so close. These walls are thin and all if'n you make me holler and I sure hope you do."

Damn, that did it. No hope in going slow this night. He placed his mouth to hers again teasing and tasting as he made short work of his coat, vest and shirt. Leona's hands ran up and down his chest. It was all he could do to kick from his boots wanting to be deep inside her.

"I ain't never felt muscles so hard, Gambler or ever touched a man like I want to touch you." She watched as he tugged his trousers and long underwear away, standing naked before her.

He scrutinized her small bed. His knee wasn't gonna like this very much, but he'd pay for that later.

"Lands, Gambler no wonder I was so sore after with that big 'ole thing of yours." She glanced away, then looked once more where he was more than ready for her.

"Some of that can't be helped to begin with but tonight's for you, Leona." He eased her to lay her across the bedding. He took her mouth, tasting her and inhaling the scent of lilac as he hovered above her.

He tugged her nightgown from her and pushed her back until she rested on the pillows. "Gods you are a beauty, Leona."

"You make me blush, Gambler." She covered her breasts by bending her arms across her chest. He eased her hands away and let his own palm run down between her breasts and lower to her belly.

"Never be shy with me, Leona, there's no need." He lay beside her and kissed her brow, the small bed creaking under his added weight. "I'll love you with all I have, like I've been trying to tell you all along."

"Gambler, still hard to believe you and me and all this lovin' like some fairy tale has come true." Her amber eyes questioned from what he could tell. "But it scared me bad when I saw that lady gambler kissing you."

"Leona, she means nothing. And our love, well, I'm not sure I have the answers on why it's so easy to love you. I don't much believe in falling in love like some fairy tale. I believe love is a choice, not something of chance. And I am going to make that choice every day when I look at you. You know I came back here to retire, give this leg some rest, maybe even give up on some things. But I never expected you, Leona. When I'm with you, you're so unassuming, just taking each breath as it comes and you make me want life again. You may me see a future I never thought I was deserving of."

"Dalton, that's about the sweetest of words I ever heard in my entire life and I'm gonna hold you to it." Her voice cracked and she brushed away tears.

He met her lips, running his hands over each of her breasts, her nipples pebbling beneath his palm. He savored her mouth and kissed his way to her breasts tasting each in soft suckles until she moaned. She was so reactive to his touch...he eased lower. He kissed her flat belly and then the juncture of her thighs.

She sucked in a startled breath. "Gambler...what're you a doin'?"

"Shhh." He lifted her leg over his shoulder and kissed her inner thighs, working his way up until he found her. He took her with his mouth, his tongue tracing the tiny bud of her pleasure. She smelled of lilacs and tasted of salt and he had waited a long time on this one.

"Gambler..." She hissed trying to writhe away from him. "That's just too much...too much....oh...."

He pinned her, lifting enough to speak. "Leona, you're gonna like this, I promise."

She gasped as he seared her again without mercy and until she was lifting to meet him.

"It's all right." He teased her again, letting is tongue and lips explore her. Her fingers moved through his hair and her sighs filled his ears. And when he eased his fingers inside her she bowed and pulled his hair making him growl as she rippled through her release with moans and sighs.

Her legs falling apart as he eased back up her body with his lips and mouth, taking a moment to tease both nipples.

He held her gaze as he rocked into her, savoring the slick warmth of her as he began the steady pushing into her. She let her hands run across his chest, her warm fingertips grazing his nipples. He stopped moving, the sensation pushing him too close. "Damn... Leona."

"You like that as much as I do and my pleasure is so nice." She moved beneath him as he fought to regain his lost focus of rhythm.

He had no words, but hell yes, he liked it. He thrust again, the old bed creaking with the impact of his pace. She opened to him and clenched tighter.

"Oh, Gambler...." She shuddered, clinging to him, reacting faster than he thought she might given her recent climax.

"Let me feel you...when it happens again." he whispered as he pinned her, wanting her body to yield. The small candle on the table flickered a silhouette of yellows across the smooth skin of her breasts as he picked up the pace. He lifted her knees and spread her further, giving her no reprieve from the hard impact her brought again and again.

Kim Turner

"Dalton..." She tensed, crying his name and taking him with her as she crossed over once more. He growled tossing his head back as Leona's body claimed him pulse after pulse. He collapsed across her at the same time the wood of the bed snapped sending them to the floor with a crash.

Leona screamed still clinging to him. He grabbed his knee with a curse as they bumped heads in the little light. He figured what had happened, but he was in no shape to do much about it and they both lay quiet.

"Gambler?" she whispered, rubbing her forehead.

"Huh?" He stifled a curse still holding his leg.

"We done broke the bed." She curled into him, holding her hand to cover her giggles.

A knock came on the far wall. "Leona? Widow Lowey called. "Are you all right in there?".

Leona sat up with a start. "Oh, yes'm just moving the table and the chair fell over."

"All right then. Get yourself some sleep," came the widow's voice again. "It's late."

"Sorry, Widow." She snuggled closer. "You hurt you knee?"

"Naahh, hurts no matter." He let go of his leg and tugged her back to him. "We already broke the bed...how about round two?"

"Gambler we might just be dangerous together if it comes down to it." She lay back, caressing him as he moved over her once more.

"I'm not opposed to a little danger." He grabbed her around the middle and flipped her over. "On your knees, beautiful woman."

****

Leona lay against Dalton, his breathing deep and

124

steady as he slept. The broken bed still lay on the floor with them in it. How did he sleep so sound while all she could do was stay awake and watch him. He was hers right now, but in a few hours, he'd have to slip away so no one would figure them.

She studied his face, the fine lines at the corners of his eyes, the trimmed beard that tickled when he kissed her. And those long dark lashes that accented his deep green eyes. Lord, but he was handsome even though he'd told her he was approaching forty years. She supposed when they were news, some would think him too old for her, but as it was, it worried her little.

Lands, but his body, hands and mouth on her had brought her pleasures she'd never known existed. No wonder Laurel, Sarah and Eliza Jane had all giggled and commented on the pleasures a man could bring. She'd reckon in their own marriage beds; they knew all about what she was a learnin'. His brought her to an intense pleasure, taking her from behind as she'd gripped the covers and cried loud into the pillows. She hadn't even known there were so many positions to try, but apparently he'd shared there was more to come. Lands, no wonder her friends smiled indeed.

But there was more than the loving part. He'd cared to talk to her from the start, even when she'd drenched his boots. And he was the first man who had ever seen beyond the clothing she hid behind, he'd even called her eyes *amber* as no one else had ever even noticed. His purchase of all the new fine clothing had been a shock at first, but she was getting used to wearing the dresses and fancier women's pants. And his words of love had caused her tears as she'd never thought herself worthy of such a thing.

He stirred with a groan. "What time is it?"

"Near abouts four," she brushed the hair back from her face.

He grimaced and rubbed his knee.

"This bed falling hurt your leg again." She rested a hand on his chest.

"Ahhh, nights never easy with it." He placed his hand on top of hers. "Not sure it was the bed, or you that done me in."

She smiled as heat warmed her cheeks. "Best you get yourself out of here a 'fore the widow wakes, though I hardly want you to go after that last round."

He chuckled. "Like that did ya'?"

"Gambler, I ain't got no idea how you seem to know my body so well. I never felt anything like when you are inside me and it comes." She kissed him wanting to touch him all she could.

"This is a start of the ways I plan to love you, Leona." He tangled his fingers in the length of her hair.

"Just never knowed there was so many ways of doin' it…ain't no women, even Laurel ever told me of that." She shook her head, "How much more we got to try?"

He brushed the hair back from her face. "I've a few more things up my sleeves. But don't forget, real love comes from here." He placed a hand over her heart. "And here." he touched her temple with his finger. It's all of it together, sharing time, loving, the simple things like a walk or a picnic too."

She giggled. "If'n, I remember right, it was that picnic that got me poked in the first place."

He put his fingers to her lips and tilted his head closer to hers. "I told you about that. I don't poke you; I make love to you."

"Making love, real love then? You and me?" She worried he might be funnin' her about his feelings and her beauty still.

"Yea, I think so." He ran a hand across his beard. "Kids gonna wonder where I been, too. But I think he's figured out a thing or two. I told him to go on to the house cause I'd be late."

"He does a good job a caring for Sable and Ernest." She ran a finger over his brow, smoothing it. "He said you were gonna get him a horse. A horse would be costin' a lot these days, given you've spent for mine and his clothes and the wood for the barn roof."

He shrugged. "I can't think of anything better to have spent it on. Oh, money makes things easier, but a man can spend a lifetime piling it up for a rainy day and die before he can spend it."

"I imagine you hadn't figured on both of us when you came back to Wylder." She whispered, his heartbeat steady in her ear as she lay across his chest.

"Nope I didn't plan for the boy to turn back up and never once expected the likes of you." He kissed the top of her head. "But I sure as hell am happy it has happened this way. I was tired of the never-ending road, didn't much like the man I had become and here I can just be me with you. But Leona, I see so many things coming back here."

"Like what?" She raised her head to look at him again, resting at his side.

"I bought you those clothes because I wanted to see you in them. I wanted to see you have pretty things and know what a beauty you are." He ran a hand down her back, his deep green eyes holding her somehow.

She gave a shiver at his simple touch, relishing in the warmth of his hand on her.

He went on. "I've wanted to settle down for a long time. Call Wylder home again and when the times right and if you're willing, I'd like to make you, my wife."

"Me your wife?" She whispered, her heart racing so hard she couldn't take another breath. "Gambler, you proposin'?"

He waited and then gave a slight shrug "If you're not opposed, once I get this game behind me and can ask you proper, would you like that?"

Leona couldn't find enough breath to make her words. He wanted her as his wife? And she'd wanted nothing more for years than to find love, real love like this. She fought the lump in her throat and swallowed hard as tears welled in her eyes and then fell. "Oh, Dalton, never thought I would ever marry but sometimes I feel like my chest is so full of you. I don't want to be apart from you any. And ain't no man ever made me cry cause I'm so happy."

"I was hopin' those are happy tears." He pulled her closer and kissed her forehead.

"Gambler you're the one man who ever knew there was more to me than I was ever willin' to show anyone else." She sniffled, though she was afraid she might burst into heavy tears. "I had to be tough, a tomboy to make it with no Pa or Ma I suppose. Guess I'm afraid of not being pretty enough for you somehow, you with your fancy dress and money and all."

He rolled her to her back and brushed the hair from her face. "Don't ever be afraid to show all of them out there just what a beauty you are, Leona. I'm not gonna be long with these games and when it's done… I want

128

you to be my wife."

"Gambler?" She whispered.

"Huh?"

"Can I just say yes now?" Heat radiated through her center with her happiness, and she held onto him as tight as she'd ever held anything.

"Absolutely."

Chapter Eleven

Dalton dismounted and tied Sable to the hitching post outside the saloon. It had been two days since he'd been to town and besides missing Leona, he needed to check with Sonny about the latest patrons who had signed up to play in the poker championship. He entered through the double doors and made his way across to the long bar.

The saloon was busy, men playing poker at the back tables, sitting to their drink with fancy ladies across their laps. A few cheers broke out at his arrival, and though he gave a nod he paid little attention to those who were all caught up in the excitement of the games.

"Town's full, Dalton, boards full too, just waitin' on one more to pay to play." Sonny set a glass before him and tossed a white cloth across his shoulder. "Drink?"

"I'll have a..." Dalton's response was interrupted.

"Sarsaparilla. Some say a man gives up the drink to keep the ghosts of his past from rushing in." A hush fell across the room, but Dalton didn't turn. He didn't have to.

Walt Cavender. And a voice he knew well.

The urge to grab his revolver was instinctive, but he'd never be fast enough. What the hell of a predicament and he should've known the man would

130

show.

"Not the only one carrying ghosts." He lifted the glass of sarsaparilla, took a sip and turned to smashed it across Cavender's shoulder. Want to get a head start, gotta do what is least expected. The glass shattered, dark liquid splashing them both. Walt Cavender's body crushed him against the bar and the man's fist caught him in the jaw. His head popped back, but he swung, catching the larger man across the brow.

"You son of a bitch," Cavender swore, bringing an elbow across his shoulder and knocking him back.

Dalton stumbled backward, but caught his stance, hopping with his bad knee. He belted a fist across the man's cheek.

He landed another punch and one to the man's face though Cavender belted him with a hard hit to the cheek, knocking him back again. About that time, Russ grabbed him as Doc Coyote took a hold on the other man.

"That's enough, both of you." Russ bellowed, keeping a tight grip on him.

Behind the bar, Sonny aimed a shotgun at Cavender.

The silence that followed was deafening as Cavender held his gaze. He should have known. He should have damn well known the bastard would surface.

He jerked free of Holt's grasp, grabbing the bar to avoid putting his full weight on his knee.

"What the hell, Cavender, waltzing in here to cause trouble." Russ shoved the man back as the Doc grabbed him again. "Save it for the table, you've no right now."

"I waited, Payne." Cavender pointed at him,

pulling free of the physician. "All these years and I'm back to take the win and kick your ass one final time." Cavender reached inside his jacket and laid cash on the bar.

"Read and sign on, then." Sonny slung a pencil and a paper before the man who never wavered as he scribbled his name and turned once more facing Dalton.

"Bring it to the game, but you start this kind of shit at the tables you'll be escorted out of town." Russ moved in between them, holding him back once more.

Cavender moseyed toward the doors, but turned. "At the tables, Payne."

Dalton glared until the man was gone, then bent to rub his knee, the bastard.

The saloon grew in noise once more, leaving him to the pain.

"The jackass come unearthed for this alone? Best you watch your back in town, Dalton. He won't be nothing but trouble." Russ turned back to him.

Dalton nodded, reaching for his cane. "He's been waitin' but it's time it seems."

"He plays a hell of a game." Holt added as he handed the cane to him. "But I'm aiming he's here for revenge if nothing more."

"No time like the present." Dalton eased weight to his leg, hopping to gain a steady gait.

"Sonny you got ice?" Coyote grabbed a towel from the bar. "Sit Payne, let me have a look."

He fell into the nearest chair, propping his foot up on another. The Doc eased his trouser leg up to expose his knee and frowned.

"The Doctor back then wanted to take the leg. Wouldn't let him, so it's as best it can be. This'll pass."

He explained though there were times he'd thought it might have been better to have lost it.

"Think you're just gonna be bruised and sore." Coyote palpated the knee enough to make him growl. "Nothing broke. Swelling at lot lately?"

He shook his head. "If I overdo it like just now. Son of a …"

The physician added a cloth with ice to his knee, holding it there. "I'd suggest stayin' off it for a few days. See how it feels. Prop it up at night on a couple of pillows. I can give you a little something for the pain."

Dalton gritted his teeth and growled under his breath. "No. Gotta have a clear head for the games, never have taken anything for it. Sometimes pains a good reminder."

Coyote eyed him closer. "You let me know."

"Thanks Doc. I'll make it." Dalton held the ice and adjusted in the chair.

Russ took a seat beside him pushing off a few spectators. "Mosey on boys give the man some air."

"You boys keep an eye out, I'm gonna take a walk, see what he's up to out there." Doctor Sullivan, checked his revolver, rolling the barrel and shoving it back into the holster at his hip.

"Careful, he can't be trusted." Russ warned as he leaned back in the chair.

"Got it." The doctor winked and walked outside not looking back.

Dalton took a deep breath. "Cavender was behind it all back then, though he's wanted revenge for his brother for a long time now. I think he never expected that or Sue Ellen taking the money."

"Seems I recall she met her own fate at the tables

later on." Russ nodded toward Sonny back at the bar. "Sonny, how about a brew."

"All right, all right, hold your horses." Sonny shouted back as he went about his work.

"Wrong end of a derringer instead of holding one. But rumor had it Cavender never found that money because she spent it." Dalton shared what he'd heard. He'd loved Sue Ellen, an outspoken woman with flaming red hair, though he'd been young at the time. But she'd double crossed them all, crushing his heart and blasting his knee out from under him.

"Well, Dalton time you play the damn game to win it once and for all." Russ offered, picking up the mug of suds Sonny set before him. "Might be the best plan."

Dalton narrowed a hard look his way. "He's keepin' score wants revenge for his brother, but I'm not playin' light."

"This town's not much studying the past. Cavender drew first. We were all here watchin'." Russ balled his fists on the table, "But not a one of us saw her draw that derringer."

Dalton held the man's gaze. That game of poker went to the wayside fast and as he killed Emmett Cavender, Sue Ellen had taken out his knee. And in the confusion, she'd made off with the money, long gone before anyone, including Walt Cavender had an inkling.

Russ leaned closer. "Tell you what. How 'bout you got a couple of days to sit idle. Rest that leg. Hell, let that little lady from the dress shop nurse you along. You'll be a knew man come game time."

"It's not like that." He offered, though it was obvious Russ Holt had figure out a thing or two. Well, he'd made little secret about his stops by the dress shop.

It was bound to happen.

"Maybe you should make it like that." Russ chuckled, and gulped his drink. "See ya' in a couple of days when the championship begins. Caleb's been planning with Daniel and Callum about the check ins and watching the doors and for cheats. You just play, what you do best."

"I knew I'd find you here Russell Holt. Had a horse to check on my rosy read rear-end." A female flurry of fancy skirts pranced toward them.

Dalton hadn't seen Adelaide Willowby in more years than he could count, but it was clear time had changed her little. She was as beautiful a woman as he'd ever seen, given her age, and it was clear she had it in for Russ.

"I suggest you bide your time to haul yourself out of this place and get your head out of that mug of beer if you know what's best." She placed her hands to her curvy hips.

Dalton still wanted to curse his knee, but this was a bit more interesting.

Russ removed his hat, already on his feet and rounding the table. "Come on Addie, just had a beer to quench my thirst. Besides I had a meeting here to handle planning of the poker championship. You already knew that."

"And the horse?" She lifted her light brows, waiting, but before Russ could answer a smile curved her painted lips. "Dalton Payne, I should've known you would still be as handsome as ever. Welcome home."

Dalton held himself steady as he stood. "It's good to see you, Miss Addie."

She turned back to Russ. "I'll expect to see you

tonight at the Social Club but you'd best make different plans if you're on a drunk, Russell." With that she sprang around on her fancy heels and pranced from the saloon, leaving behind her a few whistles and cat calls.

Russ grabbed his mug and chugged the remainder and rested his gaze on Dalton as he set it down.

"Still tenacious." Dalton stifled a grin at Russ' quick frown.

"You've no idea. Rest that leg and I'll catch up with you soon enough." With that Russ trotted from the saloon batting through the double swinging doors.

He tested his leg with another step. Hell. He'd planned to slip by the dress shop to speak to Leona but now he was a mess...dirty and his knuckles busted, his cheeks bruised right along with his pride. He took his time making it outside to Sable, not wanting the men inside the saloon to see how much pain he was in.

It took a great deal of effort to mount up and without a doubt he had a couple of rough days of recovery coming. As he urged the horse out of town, he stayed aware of those around him and that no one was following. Russ Holt was right that staying home for a bit might be the best idea.

"Son of a...." He didn't finish. This was his own fault for not expecting that Cavender would show for a poker stand-off. But his best guess was it wasn't at all about the game but more about the past and the money.

And that was the man's first mistake.

****

Leona sat on the shaded porch outside of the dress shop having her lunch break alongside Mary. The day was hot enough even after an early morning rain and the hems of her new working trousers held the mud as proof. Oh, well she could clean them when she had time to do her own clothing, later in the evening.

Mary chewed on a leftover biscuit. "It's nice you're back to work, Leona. Some days it was more than I could accomplish given the ironing and the piles of wash that never end."

"I think you did just fine. Leastwise until the widow pops her head out the door shoutin' her orders. Ain't took her long to get used to me being back, though she is a sayin' I might sew a bit soon." It was good to be back even if the widow did grumble. She broke her sandwich in half and tucked a piece into her mouth, chewing.

"And your bruises have faded. Seems Mr. Payne did a good might of caring for you." Mary dusted crackers from her skirt.

She met her friend's knowing look. "Don't know what I'd have done had he not come along when those men attacked me. Wouldn't be here I suppose."

"He's been by here to see you a lot since." Mary added with a shrug, lowering her tone. "I know it's not my place and all but...."

She narrowed her brows, not sure what to expect, but certain this was a conversation best avoided. "Just spit it out. Ain't nothin' ya can't say."

"Well, I know you're both fond of each other, but I've seen how he looks at you and a woman knows things..." Mary lowered her voice to a whisper. "I've some herbs that help keep you from becoming....with child."

Leona's mouth went dry. Could Mary or others know what she and the gambler had done? "Why you gonna go and ask me something like that?"

"Please, I mean well as you know. It's just he's come by evenings a few times to your room and... after Red...and four boys I had to find a way to help myself cause he wasn't gonna stop." Mary crossed herself, mouthing a prayer. "Not that Mr. Payne is like him, just that sometimes a woman needs to take control of things where she can, even if the Lord might not be so approvin' of it."

Leona was speechless. She supposed Mary meant well and lands, with those four wild boys she couldn't blame her for not wanting anymore young'uns. But as for herself and Dalton... a child now wouldn't be a good thing, and maybe Mary was right. "All right then...how is it done?"

Mary reached into her smock pocket and handed a pouch to her. "It's a tea I got from Lillian at the apothecary, but I don't much need it anymore. Drink the brew each evening you and Mr. Payne...well when you maybe...spend time."

Leona took the small bag, shoving it in her pocket. "I ain't a sayin' one way or another but I'll have it if the need of it comes up." She left it as best she could, though the circumstances behind the death of Mary's husband still waited in silence. Some said he'd killed himself and others suggested he'd been killed, but as it was, no one much talked of it any longer and Mary and her sons seemed to be doing well without their abusive husband and father.

Mary nodded and set her tin of water aside. "I won't say a word to anyone, you can be assured. Guess we better get back to our work."

Leona continued with her lunch. It sure was complicated when men had their willings, but Dalton had said little of it other than making sweet hints of a future together with his idea of proposing. It was strange how fast things had happened between them. One day she was pouring water on his boots and a short time later he was showing her passions she'd never know existed.

She escaped back to her pots, her heart racing at the thought. She'd never seen a grown man naked until him. But as he stood before her tall and proud with that part of him ready for her, she'd thought him a beautiful man if there were such a thing. Women always seemed to talk bad of the duties to their husband, but she'd found that once she got past the initial pain of it, she'd grown to like it. Well, she had to be blushing now, good thing she worked over the hot pots which heated her face anyway.

She turned as Gideon came running up in a breathless hurry, the kid's face red and his light hair windblown "Leona you gotta come to the homestead for a couple of days at least, Dalton's hurt that leg of his at the saloon. A big fight. Can't even walk much at all now."

"Fight?" She set the scrub board back into the water. "Catch your breath, what happened?"

"It's Dalton. Seems he got into a fight at the saloon, some man he used to know, and he hurt that leg of his, can't hardly walk none. Gideon grabbed her arm and tugged "He made it back to the homestead with Sable but it's real swollen and all bruised. Doc saw him but he barely made it back a hangin' onto Sable and can't even limp on that leg now at all.".

Mary made her way over. "Go on to him. I'll watch the pots and catch up."

She glanced around at the heap of wash still to go. "Widow's sure not gonna like this a bit. Gideon go on and get Ernest and we'll go."

The boy gave a big nod and ran to where Ernest was tied across from her room at a hitching post.

"If he's hurt, he needs you just like you needed him." Mary dunked her hands to scrub a soapy shirt. "Go on then, don't a keep him waitin."

Leona wiped her own sudsy hands and tossed the cloth aside. She turned, avoiding the mud puddles along her trot to the mule. She mounted up and offered a hand to Gideon and the boy made his way up behind her.

"Won't take no liquor to help seems." Gideon held her around the middle as Ernest took off on a canter.

"Why'd he think he could get himself back if he was injured?" She couldn't imagine him hurt and trying to ride the horse all the way home.

"Don't know. Guess he thought he had to." Gideon leaned around to look at her. "I figured you could help him on account I don't know what to do. He don't know I came for you and he might not like it much. Besides, he likes ya and... he'll feel better, you take a look at his leg and all."

She couldn't fathom what had happened. "And this was a fight at the saloon? Over the big game?"

"No, it's a man used to know Dalton. He was gonna hit Dalton but you should've seen him. Boy, does Dalton know how to fight. Punching harder than I ever seen, had that man on the ground if Mr. Holt hadn't separated them. Though I'm guessin' his leg don't bend good and all but it got bent during the fighting." Gideon flailed his fists one at a time to mimic a fight in the air.

"This was at the saloon?" She asked again, as

Dalton has forbidden Gideon to go anywhere near the place.

"Yeah, a bad fight too, men backing up and chairs flying and Dalton busted a glass over the man." Gideon made it all seem real, his blue eyes wide as saucers.

"Ain't, you supposed to be in school and not hanging around at the saloon if you want that horse?" Leona gave him a hard glare,

"Well, teacher let us out early on account its Friday." Gideon shrugged, though he continued. "And I gotta wait on him when he's not going home yet."

"Well, I'm bettin' Dalton ain't wantin' you to hang around the saloon and especially town so full of people with the game. That happens again you come find me, and you can stay helping me until he goes home." Leona warned as she urged Ernest to make the turn outside of town toward Dalton's home.

"You ain't gonna tell him, are you?" Gideon frowned, leaning around her gain. "I won't do it no more."

"Not this time, but you stay yourself out of there. Couple of men a year get hauled out of there each year shot dead." She urged the mule ahead on a trot.

"All right, but you think Dalton can still play the big game with being hurt?" The kid asked, hanging on tighter as the made the top of the rise. "That man didn't like Dalton none and I don't know how they'll play poker together. He's the last one signed on and the tables are all full up. And ain't no rooms at the hotels left they say."

"He'll play." Leona had no doubts, given his name had brought it all together. The town was busy, and shops were doing a lot of business. Banners were up for the celebration and guards were already at the bank protecting the money. "Least wise I'll see how I can help his leg, so's he can."

"All the men are a bettin' and changing their bets at times. They say Dalton will sweep the whole amount of money in no time once it starts." Gideon talked with excitement.

"Well, you just stay out of that saloon, and we'll see if we can get him well enough to play." Somehow it seemed the ride longer than any by the time Dalton's home came into view and she dismounted Ernest to run inside to him.

Chapter Twelve

Night had long closed in as Leona lay beside
Dalton in his big bed. He had slept for a few hours, she
reckoned out of sheer fatigue more than anything else.
He hadn't been happy that Gideon had brought her to
the homestead, but he had allowed her to keep cool rags
on his leg.

A small lamp beside the bed cast shadows across
Dalton's cheeks and brows. He was such a handsome
man, even sleeping. His chest was bare, the muscles
enticing her to touch though she didn't want to interrupt
his slumber. His cheek was purple where he'd been hit
in the fight, but he'd been reluctant to speak about,
telling her it was due to some happenings in his past
better left unsaid.

He moaned and his hand moved to his thigh. "You
should get some rest."

She lifted her head, resting her palm on his chest.
"Not while you need me to care for you."

He sucked in a deep breath and grimaced. "I didn't
want the boy to bother you, get the widow on you
because of your work. I'm all right, just sore."

"Mary helped. She was glad to." She let her
fingertips brush across the scattered dark hair of his
upper chest. "You've taken care of me and Gideon. Let
us see to you."

He let his hand play through the length of her hair

and her body gave a shutter.

"It's nice to lay here beside you." He held her gaze, tangling his fingers further.

"If you don't rest you won't be in the championship." She kissed his shoulder, scolding. "Never mind the other."

He drew her in for a heated kiss in spite of her thoughts. "I can play in more ways than one."

"Gambler, it scares me what happened. Gideon said it was a rough fight. How can you be at the tables if he tries again to hurt you?" She asked, her heart racing at the idea he could have been injured much worse.

"Gonna have a lot of enemies in that room, people whose money I've taken a time or two, and some who've taken mine. It's anybody's game. Walt Cavender's his name." He groaned holding his thigh. "You remember what I told you happened here in Wylder back then at the game?"

She nodded, settling closer into his side. It was so easy to want to touch him and to have him near her.

"The man I shot, Emmette Cavender, was his brother. That was self-defense, I didn't have much choice that day. He thought I had planned to take his money with the woman who shot me. I thought it was him but it was his brother." He shook his head and his lips tightened as he moved his leg.

"Walt Cavender's back for revenge then, oh Dalton." She leaned up from his embrace to look at him. He couldn't face off with a man who was after revenge could he, not in the middle of a big poker championship?

He tugged her back to him. "Not to worry, as much

144

as he wants me, it's the money he's after, cause he never got that before. She made off with it, but spent it or lost it before he ever got to her as planned. Double crossed us all."

Leona tangled her fingers with his as she lay back in his embrace. "What was her name?"

"Sue Ellen. Had us all three fighting each other all because back then I drank too much." He laughed and it rumbled through her.

"Did you love her?" The question escaped her, though she had little right to ask.

"I did, but again the alcohol blinded me to things. I should've seen long before those card games. And I've re-learned that lesson every day since she shot this knee out from under me. That's why I set a bottle close when I play, to remind me life can be fragile."

"Thank you for a tellin' me." She whispered touching his hand. He squeezed.

"I won't ever have secrets from you, Leona." He brought her hand to his lips kissing her fingers. "This will pass, but I am glad you came, though I'm gonna kick Gideon's hind end if he doesn't stay away from the saloon."

"I think he just wants to see what you're doing; he admires you and is happy here…and so am I." She shivered then as he turned her palm to his lips.

He eased her from him and tugged her over his chest again, kissing her. "Sit atop me, Leona, won't have to move much that way."

"Dalton, your knee…" She protested as he teased the buttons to her new work blouse and played his hands under her chemise.

"It'll be sore regardless…" He pulled her shirt

away and his hands massaged her back all the way to her trousers. "Take these off, let me watch."

It amazed her how fast her pulse raced and her nipples perked. He was warm and yes, she wanted him to love her…. but…

She stood from the bed and lowered her trousers and pantaloons, aware he was watching. "God, Leona, you are so beautiful and not a man in Wylder would have ever known it, but I knew." He took her hand and eased her to sit astride him. "Rest on your knees."

"Well, we ain't a done it like this a 'fore…" She shifted and he eased her down, taking her full and hard.

She tossed her head back at his entry, biting her bottom lip to allow it.

"Just move slow…" His face distorted as he showed her the motion. "Just like that."

He leaned back as she rocked, though she was awkward at first. He found her breasts and filled each palm, squeezing and touching her nipples until she shivered and moaned.

She quit moving, breathless and uncertain how her body was to do what it did atop him.

"No, don't stop, ride…. let me watch you, Leona…" Sweat beaded his brow as his fingers found her. She hissed as he stroked her there and she rocked again and again.

"That's it…let me feel you…" His hands found her hips and smoothed over her bottom as she moved with purpose, holding his shoulders to keep her balance. "Give it to me, Leona, all for me…"

"Ahhhh…" She clenched tight as he pulled her down and held her to him, his own body bucking and shuddering with her as he came.

He collapsed back to the bedding taking her with him, both of them breathless and clinging to each other.

"Gambler, I'm afraid I can't marry you..." She rolled beside him.

"Why's that?" He brushed her hair back from her face.

"Cause if we marry and we poke...make love, like this all the time, I ain't gonna survive it at some point." She closed her eyes and opened them once more.

He chuckled, "Well, let's get married anyway and I'll make it my priority to see that you survive it each and every time."

"Promise you will be careful, Dalton, because I don't want to have you hurt or worse." She squeezed his hand.

"I promise." He wrapped both arms around her and Leona held onto him wishing dawn would be slow in its arrival.

****

Leona placed a hot iron to a pair of bitches on her long drying board. The work today was busier than ever, the town bustling with people arriving for the poker championship. She gazed into the afternoon sun and then smiled as Laurel pulled her carriage to a stop at the dress shop.

"*Yee-ona*!" Jesse, Laurel's son, climbed down from the wagon and came running to her, Harold, the chicken close on his heels.

"Jesse, boy, aren't you gettin' so big these days?" She scooped up the little boy as Laurel ambled up carrying two baskets of clothing. Since her marriage to Caleb Holt, Laurel had taken home the mending from the dress shop along with creating new clothing she returned each week. It was only about one day each week she stayed on at the dress shop.

"Town's so busy what with the big game beginning." Laurel sat both baskets one at a time on the table, rubbing her rounded belly. "I've finished all the sewing I've taken home, back for more."

"Widow figured you to be back by today." Leona put Jesse back down. "Stay away from those pots, Jesse, they're hot."

Jesse giggled as he climbed up to the dress shop porch, Harold clucking alongside. "Harold hungry, Mama."

Laurel handed Jesse a small brown bag from the top of one of the baskets. "You sit right there with Leona and you and Harold have a cookie while I hang the clothing inside." She dug in the baskets, lifting several longer items and draping them across her arms.

"Yes, Mama." Jesse shoved a cookie into his mouth, giving the rooster a few crumbles from the bag.

"Afternoon, Laurel." Mary greeted from the ironing board, opposite porch from them.

"Hello, Mary," Laurel answered as she hung several dresses inside and returned.

The Widow Lowery followed her with a new armload of items. "These finer dresses are for the social club. Seems that Miss Addie is planning that the whores entertain all those no goods arriving to town, shame to us all." The widow fanned herself and handed the garments to Laurel as she stepped to the ground again.

"Thank you, Widow Lowery, I'll have these back promptly." Laurel nodded, carrying new items in the baskets to her waiting wagon.

"See that you do, dear." The widow pointed toward

town. "It's busier by the day with that poker championship starting soon. And it isn't that anyone can sleep with those no good shootin' their weapons all night long. I personally will be glad when it's all over."

"Caleb mentioned every hotel and boarding house is full as far as Cheyenne and a lot of surrounding cities." Laurel added as she returned placing her hands on her hips, supporting her back.

"Well, the first of the big games begins in a few minutes, right at noon. I expect it might be a lot more people arrive to town just to watch in the coming days." Leona stirred one of the pots, mindful that Jesse was still on the porch.

"Daniel said some men are camped down by the river since no rooms are open anywhere. He and Callum were riding through there a few days back." Sarah spoke from the doorway, an embroidered smock in her hands.

"Well, this whole town is making money, no matter the devil's hand in it." The widow leaned on the doorway, taking a handkerchief to wipe the sweat from her neck. "You ladies keep at your work, more's waiting."

Leona met Laurel's gaze and they both smiled as she turned back to her work. Some things never changed. The poker tournament would begin at noon and while she hadn't seen Dalton today, his knee was better, and he'd already be here in Wylder if she were guessing right.

"They've banned guns from the saloon and the sheriff is telling the men no shooting will be tolerated once the train whistle starts the play. If so, they get arrested and kicked right out of town." Leona added what Dalton had told her as she tossed in three more shirts to the pot of whites. "Course some of 'em probably already loaded up on the spirits."

"If you ask me, sheriff needs to keep the town of Wylder in line like that all the time." The widow shook her head. "You ladies mind your work; I've rounds to make at the hotels and the Social Club with Laurel bringing back the finished dresses." The widow turned inside the shop once more.

With the widow gone, Laurel wiped her brow in the already staggering heat. She sat beside Jesse as the rooster flew to the grass and began to peck at the ground.

"How's Dalton's knee? Russ told me and Caleb about what happened." Laurel asked as she folded the empty cookie bag Jesse had set aside.

Leona stepped back from the pots and ran the iron down a pair of britches. "I checked on him again yesterday. He's a mite better, ready to play I suspect."

"He was at the ranch recently, asking Caleb about a horse." Laurel rubbed a hand to her belly. "He's a very nice man, very kind to Jesse and good to animals from what I see."

"He's promised Gideon a horse if he stays in school like he should." She turned the britches the other direction and swiped the hot iron over them again.

"Seems he thinks a lot of you, too." Laurel angled a hard glance at her.

Sarah lowered her embroidery and Mary stopped pushing the iron across her board.

Leona narrowed her sights to each of them in turn. Well, She could always count on her friends to call her out. "Well, ain't this some fine bit of being rather nosey?"

"Oh, we mean well, Leona." Laurel got up and eased a bit closer "My goodness, look at how you dress now, even just to work. Fancy trousers and a pretty blouse. Just beautiful and it seems Mr. Payne knows it too."

Leona figured her friend did mean well, but it didn't keep the heat from her cheeks. "Well, he's a nice man is all." She gave in. "And he and I are courtin' though I ain't a needin' that gossip to make the quilting circle at the social club."

"Leona." Laurel gave her a quick hug "I think you deserve a bit of happiness as it is. We're not making fun; we care about you, and he is a very handsome man."

Sarah stepped closer to the edge of the porch. "And we do want you to be happy, never seen you smile like you do when he comes by here. Mary and I both think so."

Mary offered a knowing nod.

She glanced at each of them. None of them could know that she had already shared the Gambler's bed, or he had shared and broken hers. And what would they all think if they did? She supposed they had all figured out her secret but weren't saying anything. "Well, if you all must know we've been on a picnic of where he kissed me. Mind you that's all and we gone as far as for me to give him a run for his money at a hand of poker, playing right there at his table and I sure enough beat him." She set the cooling iron down and folded the britches. "And he was far impressed with that, surprised my daddy taught me the game so well and all. But other than that, y'all need to quit a gawking and figurin' on a gossipin' about something else."

"Be happy Leona. Life is so very short, and we all just adore you." Laurel gave her hand a squeeze. "Come, Jesse, time to go."

"I'll be back in a few days, much luck I hope to Mr. Payne in the championship." Laurel helped Jesse and the rooster into the buggy and then eased herself up and inside.

Leona grabbed another hot iron and a man's long sleeve blue shirt, tossing it on the board. She peered across town which was busy with people filling the board walks and the streets. Dalton would be at the saloon by now since the poker championship would begin soon.

He'd told her he was never sure of a win though he was confident he would play up until the final few games. Her stomach quivered, anxious for him to do well.

And while she wasn't sure, she suspected he was wearing that fine suit with the shiny boots she'd poured water over when she first met him. Well, win or not, he'd be the most handsome of the men in the room and of that she hadn't a single doubt.

Chapter Thirteen

Dalton scanned the saloon as patrons of the big poker championship checked in and took their seats. The game, which would last for days, was about to begin. He took his chair at the table he'd been assigned as the first train whistle blew. Sonny had set up with the train depot to sound the train engine whistle so it could be heard all throughout Wylder.

This first of the games would be with each player holding their chips and over the day of play, some would lose their small fortunes and be forced to walk away. The town was bustling with people, and word had it hotels and boarding houses had been filled to capacity for days. So Wylder had its championship and he'd been smart enough to grab two rooms at the Vincent House Hotel so he could stay in town.

He'd been searched like all the rest for hidden cards and weapons. He glanced at the clock and around at the other tables of players. About thirty seconds remained for the empty chair across from him to be filled. There was a hustle of chatter, with Sonny beaming from his post on the ladder holding a bell.

Across the saloon, Russ and Caleb searched each patron on entry, even those who would sit in the small galley of watchers. Daniel and Callum were armed and manned the front and back entrances of the saloon, leaving the sheriff to handle things on the streets of

Wylder.

Cheers erupted as the last patron made his entry. Leo Castle dashed into the saloon and flopped into the empty chair. He was breathless but wearing a smile as he stood again to be searched by Russ.

The old rancher chuckled. "Barely made it kid, but take your seat."

"Yes, Sir. Mornin' Gentleman, Leo Castle." He spoke with a nod to those at his table.

Dalton leaned back as the chips were placed before each player who had paid to play. Well, it was here. The moment of truth and the beginning of another championship game, something he thought he'd put behind him for good. It had ended up with fifteen tables with five players at each table. He glanced at his chips accustomed to scanning the amount for accuracy which he found there.

He glanced around the room. Oh, they'd all shown, including Lefty Parsons, who sat at a corner table with a scowl across his face. Mid-room was Edward Locke, who dusted his fine sparkling suit. The steel tycoon all smiles. Next table over, Alice O'Hare and all her feathers were entertaining the men before her. Some things never changed.

Near the saloon doors, Gordon Conroy had checked in and took his chair, saying not a word to anyone. He'd handed his revolver to Russ with a glare. And at the next table Elias Littlefoot, the half breed Sioux, had entered amidst a few jests. That an Indian was allowed to play riled some, but the rules didn't exclude anyone from play as was his preference. Earlier, Poncho Gonzalez had made his rather loud entrance, handing off his own weapons and cheering himself as he swigged from a bottle of tequila.

Dalton adjusted his leg and lifted his gaze to Walt Cavender's hard glare. He held his poker face, both men in a stand-off of sorts, not broken until another man stood from his seat blocking them from each other. Well, let the damn game begin then.

"Welcome to the beginning of the Wylder Poker Championship, biggest game in these here parts in more years than we can all count." Sonny raised his voice to carry over the cheers from outside the saloon. "Looks like all the seats are now filled and I'll remind you of the rules of this set of games. But first, gentleman, and madam." He glanced at Alice O'Hare and back to the men in the saloon.

"You folks are playing a professional game for the pot of one hundred thousand dollars to the top winner. Fifty-thousand to the player placing second, and twenty-five-thousand to third place." He waited for the noise to die down before continuing. "I'll remind you that cheating will not be tolerated, nor will any weapons or you'll forfeit your money and be escorted out of town."

"There will be no leaving the game during play, or the game will be forfeited. Each participant will play until they lose their funds in full or quit. Each game will begin with a lottery draw of who sits at each table in that order." Sonny hopped up to the bar and turned to face them again. "Because of the large amount of money invested by each player, if a player becomes ill or injured or for some reason is unable to play the game, a second may be named to sit in your chair to continue the game of play, but this rule can be used once for one replacement."

Dalton eyed the other men at the table. None of the three were men he knew. One was already nervous, fidgeting and bouncing a leg. The other sat stoic and carried a deep scar across his brow. Another wore a top hat that Russ had searched and plopped back onto his head. He guessed they wouldn't last long in a game like this, given their appearance and the fact he didn't know them. But next to him, Frederick Baldwin, railroad tycoon, held a silly smile and sized up each player as well.

"And now players…on the ready…" Sonny rang the bell. Let the games begin."

Frederick Baldwin was handed the deck at his table, "Gentlemen, ante up."

Each player laid down the required ante at the center of the table in turn.

Dalton touched the breast pocket of his coat where the flask remained. Somehow it wasn't there any longer to remind him about his inability to hold his liquor. But it did steady him to be cautious and give the game his best. And while most were taking up with whiskey and beer, he and the kid along with Alice abstained as did several others.

Baldwin shuffled and laid the deck before Dalton who cut without a word. The man lifted the cards again and dealt in the proper fashion.

Dalton didn't lift his cards but took a look at each of the men at his table. Shaky leg didn't move and blinked hard then continued to fidget. One down, he had nothing. Beside him, top hat shook his head back and forth. Frederick adjusted his collar. Big mistake, nothing there either. But Scar sat forward, eager.

He picked up his hand. Strange after all these

years, he never was unnerved by the cards. A pair of tens. He discarded three cards and drew three more.

As luck would have it, he'd drawn another ten. Three of a kind. He scrutinized each player as they each drew their cards. The leg shaker made the table rock catching the attention of them all as he laid his cards down folding with a scowl.

Dalton kept his hands steady as the men each took their turn. Baldwin bluffed and stayed in the game.

Scar laid down one card and drew another, his face unchanging.

Dalton narrowed a hard gaze on the mans' card and there it was, the tell-tale sign of marked cards. He should've seen it coming given the men he was playing when it came down to it.

Frederick tugged his collar and looked from one to the other. "I'm out, Gentlemen, this first game, more than a bit of figuring us each, would you say?"

No one answered him but across the room, cheers erupted as several tables gained their winners.

Dalton made a half pot size bet, more than appropriate for being this early in the game.

It held quiet between him and the man with the scar as top hat gave into the loss and folded. The game continued for some time, Scar slowing things down.

"Mr. Payne, I'm afraid I have to call." Scar waited his eyes showing little.

Dalton never dropped the man's gaze as he motioned Russ closer. "No need."

Scar narrowed his gaze. "I said call!"

"Sir, I won't be honoring your request. You got a couple of marked cards in your hand there." The room fell silent around them.

"You calling me a cheat?" The man started to stand but Russ pushed him back to his chair.

Dalton lifted his cane and flattened the man's hand to the table with the force of the brass handled end, spilling his cards. "That's right."

Scar cursed, but he was pinned.

Russ picked up the hand and inspected the reverse side of the cards with a nod at the scratch marks within the artwork. The first just a tad down from the top edge, the second halfway down the card. It being obvious that the first represented the King he held, the second his nine. "Sure enough, get this piece of trash out of town."

Scar didn't say a word as Caleb dragged him from the table and out the swinging doors to the crowd that erupted in whoops and laughter.

Dalton pulled his cane to his side once more. He had an eye for cards that had been tampered with, though Scar did a good job of what he'd tried. The hints were so small and hidden in the artwork of the back of the cards not many would have spotted it. He sipped a sarsaparilla placed before him and settled back into his chair.

So Wylder had its first win, but the intensity was about to increase and the first day of play was far from over.

****

Leona opened the door to the room at the Vincent House Hotel. She'd never been inside anywhere but the back entrance for dropping off and picking up laundry. But after his first game this morning, Dalton had found her at the dress shop, kissed her and shoved a key into her hand. His quick whisper was urgent, and he'd let her know he'd done well in the first round but had things to take care of before the next set of play.

He'd insisted she dress her best and go on to the hotel as soon as her work was done. So, she'd hurried to bathe, put on the fancier of her new dresses and made her way there. And she now closed the door of the room behind her.

She stood in awe of the fanciful place, with scarlet draperies that matched the bed coverings and as fine of furniture as she'd ever seen anywhere before. There was ample space and even a real rug along the stained hardwood flooring. She blinked and touched the fine lamp on the table, turning up the flame and admiring the oversized clean room. There wasn't a doubt Dalton would visit her later in the night, though she was certain he'd known to keep that very quiet. She'd sure be the talk of the town if word got out about this and she hadn't even told any of the other women at the dress shop. She couldn't recall ever having stayed in any hotel.

Dalton had a second room for him and Gideon, making it a bit easier to hide their secret should anyone ask. Well, she was a bundle of nerves being in such a fine place. She wanted to giggle. A real hotel and another night of Dalton's pleasures. Lands he had a voracious appetite for her, and she had grown fond of it herself, no matter they weren't married. But she supposed her Pa, should he have known this would be disappointed, but he was long gone and she was making her own way to happiness.

She glanced at the fancy clock on the wall. The poker championship would be ongoing for hours yet. It seemed players would be at their table until their money was lost and that could take a while. As Dalton explained, some games took longer than others and as they progressed would slow even more.

Gideon let her know Dalton had played well in the morning rounds, bringing in more chips than the others at his table. She'd warned him to stay away from the saloon, but it seemed he and a few of the older boys from school had done their best to watch through the side windows. She supposed curiosity was natural at that age, as she herself had found it hard to work her shift. She was thankful Mary would be covering Saturday and Sunday, leaving her weekend in this fine hotel with Dalton. The good thing was in her current fancy dress, no one would have much paid notice to her as the Leona they knew.

She began unpacking her things, laying the items in the fine cedar drawers in a real chest. She ran a hand along the fine wood and then walked to the window to open it for a bit of fresh air.

The sun was setting, darkness in the distance but town was full of people walking the streets. She was fidgety and couldn't keep one single thought without another. She was sure it wasn't the games that had her on end as much as the idea of lying in this fancy bed with Dalton later on. Her body could react in a second thinking about the ways he touched her.

She turned to a knock at the door, thinking it could be Gideon if anyone. She eased the door back. "Yes."

"We've the meal you ordered, Ma'am." A bell hop dressed in a box hat pushed a cart of food past her, setting it up at the small cherrywood table that had two chairs.

"Well, I…all right." She started to protest as she'd not ordered any food. But it was most likely Dalton who had ordered the meal. She inspected the delicacies, steaming pieces of pink meat and potatoes in a fancy sauce and long green beans as bright as a field of grass. And a pie so fancy it didn't look real with its high white swirls of meringue.

"Thank you." She nodded as the boy made his way into the hallway and closed the door. She turned back to the food, touching the slender pieces of pink meat she'd never seen the likes of before.

The door eased open again and Dalton closed it behind him, wearing a wide grin.

"A penny for your thoughts, beauty." He removed his black hat and set it aside as he drew her close for a kiss.

Leona allowed the kiss but then pulled away. "How was the game? Dalton this room, never seen anything so fancy. I won't even be able to sleep it's so pretty."

He chuckled and held her closer still. "Wasn't planning on letting you sleep."

Heat rushed her cheeks even if she was hoping the same. "Did you win?"

"I am a winner with you, woman." He whispered, nibbling at her ear. "Yes, played against Gordon Conroy. He pulled a knife on another who cheated, had somehow hidden it in the leather of his boot. Both of them got hauled out by Russ and Caleb, leaving me to play against Edward Locke. The man knows his game, but he tried bluffing. I didn't believe him and took him with a full house, but the queen of hearts is all mine." He kissed her slow and searing, leaving her knees weak as wash water. How was it he did that, making her body fill with a quick passion of heat riding between her thighs?

"All yours, Gambler." She wrapped her arms around him with so much ease.

"But first," He angled a nod toward the table taking her hand. "Hungry, madam?"

She allowed him to lead her to the table. "You're a limping more with your knee."

"It's just hard to sit and not fidget with it, but it'll get a rest a bit later." He held out a hand and pulled out her chair.

"Lands, Gambler, you make me feel like a queen or something. This is very expensive." She protested, though the smile he wore said this was all for her. "Ain't ever had a meal like this."

He took his seat, letting go of her hand. "We've got the finest players in poker around those tables, all the towns in excitement and I wanted to treat you to this for now, a real nice room and…" he motioned to the food. "A taste of the ocean, had it sent here for you, Leona."

Her mouth fell open. "A taste of the ocean, what is it?"

"Shrimp, a delicacy on both coasts." He lifted one, pulled its remaining tail off and dipped it into a white sauce and waited on her. "It's from the sea."

Leona lifted one and did the same. "Looks about like a crawdad from the creek if'n you ask me, not sure I should eat it. Good for fishing though."

"Go on, it's chewy and fresh. It's supposed to be cool but a bit sweet if you taste it." He chewed the shrimp and sat the tail of it on the side of his plate.

She followed alike, at first a bit put off. "Well, it is sweet."

"Try another." He offered and watched as she did.

"So, tell me about the games and all, it's hard

wondering all day how you're a doing." She took a sip of tea, and coughed and sputtered. She grabbed her napkin. That was not tea, it was spirits if she knew anything about it.

"Oops…" Dalton handed her his napkin, too. "Slow down girl, that's red wine, the finest the hotel had to offer."

"Wine…" She coughed again, her throat on fire. "It 'bout choked me, Gambler. I ain't ever taken part in any spirits, 'ceptin that night I was beaten. I thought it was tea."

"It's all right, catch your breath, wine is to be sipped, not gulped. You're a lady, small sips." He offered.

"Now you tell me." She cleared her throat still trying to catch her breath.

He shrugged and held her gaze once more. "I just want to show you nice things, Leona. I didn't mean to get you all choked. It's an acquired taste."

"Acquired taste, huh. It's a bit like spoiled apples. But I do like the shrimp. So that Conroy pulled a knife?" She took another bite of the curled pink thing from the ocean.

He sipped the water. "Yep, he pulled a knife from the leather in his boot, but Caleb Holt had a gun right on him. Both kicked from the championship money lost."

Leona chewed another shrimp and lifted the wine to show him she was sipping this time. It was so strong; she couldn't figure why so many folks liked it, but she was being cultured one step at a time by the man before her. "You bluffed him then?"

"Yep, but then he pulled his weapon. Big mistake."

He took up another shrimp. "God, you are beautiful, Leona, the best part of my day."

"You are changing the subject." She grinned and relished in the warmth spreading across her cheeks. "What'd you do with Gideon?"

He angled a glance at her sitting his napkin aside. "He's already asleep in the next room."

"Two rooms, Gambler…thought this one was big enough." She sipped the wine again, the taste becoming tolerable.

"I told you, I wanted you to have the opportunity to stay in a nice room. I'll be here for a bit, but I'll sleep in the next room, so no one can know anything about us. And as for Gideon, I need to keep him here and not running to the homestead and all over town. Seen him and some other boys watching from the side window at the saloon today." He gave a slight chuckle.

"I warned him to keep out of there." She blinked and smacked her lips which were beginning to tingle.

"I suppose it's natural for the boys to be rather curious, but there's a lot of roughies in town. Don't want either of you hurt." He wiped his mouth and sat the napkin back down.

"How come I got my own room here to make it convenient for you?" She lifted her brows, feeling a bit lightheaded from the wine. She giggled, not even knowing she was going to do so and then giggled again.

"That's the idea, though I want you to stay here all weekend and order food when you're hungry and take a long hot bath in the smell good stuff a couple of times if you like. Enjoy this." He held a smile, watching her for a moment.

"All right then."   She giggled yet again and

hiccoughed. "I've enjoyed this meal for sure. Now what?"

"And now…" Dalton got up and went to her. He bent and kissed her, tasting her lips and hugging her to his body as he helped her up. "You taste like the wine."

"Do I?" She asked as he eased her dress from her shoulder, letting it puddle at her feet. His mouth on her bare skin made her swoon every time and she leaned into him as he worked the ties to her stays moving them toward the big bed.

"Had to make myself focus on the game today, but it was all I could do to keep this from my mind." He grinned as he turned her and tackled the stays.

"Won't tell you I wasn't a thinking about it, too." She added, another giggle and a slight burp. "Sorry. I meant pardon me, please."

Her stays fell away with her chemise, leaving her chest naked. The gambler was good at undressing her with ease, and with her breasts bared, his hands found each from behind her.

She shuddered, wondering if it was the wine or his touch. "Dalton…"

"Shhhh, let if feel nice." He turned her and eased her across the bed, her legs hanging off the side as he removed his shirt and stepped from his trousers, his body more than ready.

He hovered over her and eased her pantaloons away, kissing her thighs as he removed her boots and stockings, leaving her naked. She giggled again as he kissed her and then began at her breasts, teasing each of her nipples, and then his hand playing into her center making her writhe in the pleasure she anticipated.

She sighed as his fingers teased her there, where

she wanted his touch. "Lands, Dalton…"

And then he joined her, holding her legs about him as he still stood, pushing deeper with each stroke. And this time her body took him without the pain, and she moved to meet him each time he thrust into her. He groaned and upped his pace, harder and faster.

Leona wrapped her legs about him, but he bent her knees, pushing them higher, spreading her as he filled her. She hung onto him as the hints of pleasure teased her and until with each impact of his body she sighed in the heated pleasure.

"Give me all of you, Leona…" He leaned close to her face taking her lips and she cried into his mouth when the pleasure came for them both.

He moaned and her body pulsed hard with each stroke he gave her and somehow, they were one for a time, each to rising to the pleasure of the other.

He moved beside her hugging her to his large warm body as he whispered. "Gods, Leona, I'm gonna say it this time, I love you, woman, like I've never loved another."

Leona's head whirled even though she didn't move but nausea took her. "Gambler?"

"Huh?"

"The room is spinning. I think I'm a gonna be sick." She closed her eyes and tried not to retch.

"Sleep, that way you won't be sick." He brushed her hair back with a bit of care.

"Sorry, I am gonna be…" She rolled to lean over the side of the bed as Dalton scrambled to place the basin on the floor. She fought it but it came anyway, her head spinning as she lost the content of her belly.

"Oh, Gambler, I'm gonna die…" She fell back

against the pillows. Moments later, Dalton placed a cool rag to her face and mouth.

"Just rest." He whispered and kissed her forehead. "You won't die, I promise."

She thought about it, "Gambler, I might feel better if'n I did, 'cept I do love you and think I won't die just yet."

He laughed and lay back down with her. "I'll be right here till you sleep."

"Gambler?" She couldn't even whisper, afraid to move.

"Huh?"

"At least I didn't toss my turnips on your boots." She giggled but then stopped, holding her spinning head.

"Nope, you sure didn't. Close your eyes, Leona." He chuckled again, the warmth of his body a comfort. She wasn't sure as she let go but thought she smiled before the sleep took her down to a spinning darkness of comfort.

Chapter Fourteen

Dalton pulled the black ribbon tie through the collar of his shirt, watching in the fancy mirror as he shaped it to have the tails hang the proper length. He'd risen in the early dawn, leaving Leona to her slumber, and eased into the room he shared with Gideon.

Across the room the boy watched him with keen interest. "I don't know why you have to dress so fancy just for poker, seems a waste not to dress in comfortable clothes so you can think."

He finished with the tie and eyed the boy where he sat to his breakfast at the small fancy table. "Well, take a look at yourself."

"Me." Gideon inspected his new brown trousers, long sleeve tan button shirt and leather suspenders, even glancing at the new brown boots.

Dalton walked closer to him. "You're dressed nice and in school each day you look handsome and well taken care of. How are the other children treating you there now?"

The lad shrugged, taking a glance at his clothing once more. "Fine, I reckon."

"And what about in town?" Dalton nodded toward the window where outside, Wylder was already waking, the sun over the rise adding a yellow glow to the room.

"What do you mean?" Gideon shrugged, fidgeting in his chair.

"The people. I'll bet they are much nicer to you now that you present respectable. A lot different than when you go off that train in tattered pants and a torn shirt." Dalton waited, giving him time to let his words sink in. "A lot different than the boy hunting a job no one would give him."

"I guess so." Gideon popped a sausage in his mouth.

"Gideon, people will treat you how you allow them to. My Pa taught me that early on, but I learned as a young man, just like any businessman, dress for the win. In fact, dress like you already won. The men in business wear their fine suits for the same reasons. And people believe what they see." His father had made sure he always had decent clothing and spoke well to people with respect.

"Even works for Leona, too." A smile spread across the boy's face.

Dalton's brows narrowed. "Leona?"

"Sure. She's doing the same work a washin' all those clothes but all girled up in them fancy dresses you got her. All the men in town are lookin' at her when they pass by, and some are coming by the dress shop on purpose seems." He giggled and he stuffed eggs into his mouth, talking as he chewed. "She's got the widow a chasin' them all off with a broom most of the time."

Dalton wasn't sure at all how he felt about that. "A woman should know what it's like to wear pretty things and hear pretty words. Always remember that when you grow up."

Gideon studied him for a long moment. "That's where you were last night...in her room?"

Well, he hadn't expected that. He gulped hard.

"Yes, and I treated her to a very nice dinner and conversation. Not sure Leona has had the opportunity to enjoy a hotel, much like you." Dalton brushed his vest of a bit of lint.

The kid pushed again. "But you stayed late..."

"Talking. Women like that sort of thing, for a man to spend time chatting over a lot of things they are interested in." He tucked the small flask of bourbon into his jacket pocket.

"Well, these walls are thin, sounded a bit more than just talking." The boy went back to his food. "Ain't no secret and all. Used to hear him with my Mama, if he was drinking, he beat her too."

Dalton had figured much of the story prior to the boy's nod. "Gideon not all men are like him."

How the hell did he explain this one? "Look, Leona and I have grown to care for each other and as soon as these games are out of the way, I plan to officially ask her to be my wife. I'd never hurt her like that, nor would I ever lay a hand on you. Come here, let me show you something."

He pulled a small velvet pouch from his pocket. "Take a look at this."

Gideon moseyed over and whistled. "That's a real diamond, ain't it?"

"Isn't it." He corrected and continued. "When the times right, gonna get down on my good knee and ask her proper, like a lady deserves." His pulse raced at the idea, but somehow, he was more than ready.

"Maybe she won't like it much I'm there at the homestead, if you go and get married." Gideon turned away, sitting back at the table.

Dalton shook his head, placing a hand to Gideon's

170

shoulder. "What did I tell you about the homestead?"

The boy lifted his gaze. "That it was my home as long as I wanted it to be."

Dalton tousled his hair. "That's right. If Leona accepts my proposal, it's still your home and she knows that."

He nodded, shoving a forkful of eggs into his mouth.

"Now you get on to the things I've asked of you. Check on Sable and Ernest at the livery, then come back here and get to your homework and tonight maybe we'll play a little of our own cards here for fun." Dalton brushed his jacket sleeves and studied himself in the mirror once more. "But I best not see you lingering in the window watching the games at the saloon."

"Awe..." Gideon protested, twirling his fork on his plate. "Just watchin' ain't hurtin' nothing. Me and the other boys can see pretty well from that upper window."

"Go on." He handed the boy his hat. "Be on your way."

The kid lopped the hat on his head and grabbed another sausage. "Dalton?"

"Yeah?"

"Some of the kids at school keep asking if you're my Pa and... well, I don't know what to say to 'em but if my name is Gideon Payne, shouldn't I call you that?" Gideon's wide blue eyes didn't blink, not once. "Pa, I mean?"

"Would you like that?" Dalton swallowed the knot in his throat and maybe soon a family with he and Leona.

"Sure would...Pa." The smile that lit the boy's face

stretched ear to ear as he took off out of the hotel room.

"Hey, walk." Dalton shouted down the hallway after him, but Gideon was already gone. He shook his head as he turned back into the room. "Pa....it has a ring to it."

He grabbed the two keys off the dressing table and went back out into the hallway and opened Leona's door, slipping inside.

She still lay on her side, the heavy covers over her as he'd left her earlier. He leaned down and kissed her pouting lips, waking her.

She moaned. Her hair was a mess but what a beauty she was, still naked. She drew the covers tighter. "Oh, Gambler....mmmmmmhhhh." She held a palm to her head. "My head's gonna pop right off my shoulders."

"It's the wine. I should've known better than to give it to you." He grabbed a cloth and dipped it into cool water, wringing it. "Here." He laid it across her forehead.

"This isn't good, Gambler. The whole room is spinning." She whispered, never opening her eyes.

"Just sleep it off. I am sorry. I'm heading into town for a bit and the game whistle will blow five of nine. I'll see you tonight." He kissed her forehead.

She whimpered keeping her eyes closed. "I won't be here cause I'll be dead. But you can go ahead and plan my funeral if you like. I ain't ever taking spirits again."

He gave a chuckle and rested a hand on her back. "Oh, you'll die one day an old lady in a warm bed but not like this. He kissed her cheek. I'll check on you after the first of the games are done and make sure you're still among the living though."

She groaned. "Gambler?"

"Huh?"

"Last night, what I remember of it…" She moved the cloth on her eyes and looked at him and of all things smiled. "Thank you for the nice hotel where I can lay here and die in a fancy bed having been loved well."

He kissed her once more, giving a hearty laugh. "You're not gonna die, Leona, but I am glad you would have done so happily."

"Gambler?" She lifted her head to look at him. "Win."

****

The afternoon of poker play had taken time and patience in the heat inside the saloon. Smoke lingered in the air as well as the stalemate of various liquors. Dalton laid down his hand, the call made by Elias Littlefoot. He'd done a good job of gaining a hand he didn't need to bluff about, but he'd done well in making it seem he had bluffed. Eights full of Kings.

A full house had taken the hand, knocking several from the game with the loss of all their chips. Things were narrowing down.

The Indian stood and nodded in respect. "It's the way of the game, and as usual well played."

"Indeed." He'd had always liked Elias and had played him at various events over the years when the Sioux had been allowed.

Easing up, Dalton checked the far window. Gideon peeked in with a few other boys. He lifted his brow and the boy disappeared, leaving him to chuckle. It was nearing three and he needed to check on Leona.

Making his way on foot to Hank's place he went

inside and purchased a sandwich for himself and a small bowl of broth for Leona. He'd asked the hotel staff not to disturb her. She needed the rest and the fewer who noticed her, the less talk that might hit the quilting circle.

He walked along the street with a few nods to cowboys giving him encouraging shouts. But when he turned the corner, Walt Cavender stepped out before him. He wasn't surprised in the least, though he hadn't had his guard up.

"Payne. Looks like old times coming to those tables." Cavender spoke louder than necessary, as if he wanted to draw attention from those who gathered around them.

He held the man's gaze, the revolver on his hip riding heavy. He set the food aside on the porch of the business beside them.

"Awe... just like before and come that last table whistle...it'll be as it should be. Towns don't forget Payne and neither do brothers." The man stepped closer in challenge.

"Emmette drew first, but it seems neither of you got the payoff you were planning." He pushed back in defense.

"You know, Payne, I'll never understand it." Cavender narrowed his gaze. "She loved you with a passion, didn't even want to do it so she took out that knee of yours instead of killing you as planned. How's the leg holding up these days?"

Dalton didn't move, but held steady. He'd loved Sue Ellen or at least at the time he had, but she'd double crossed them all.

"That's right, she was supposed to take you if

Emmett didn't, but she just couldn't do it. She met such an ugly and well-deserved end I might add." Cavender laughed as he pulled his jacket open, tucking it behind his gun belt.

That was it. Dalton stepped closer. "Best you step aside, Cavender."

Russ Holt eased between them, holding his hands up. "Gentleman. Save it for the game."

The stand off held for a moment longer as he held Cavender's narrowed gaze.

"See you at the tables, Payne." Cavender turned toward the saloon once more belting out with laughter, which was odd.

He grabbed the food once more.

"Best you sidestep that one, Dalton. Watch yourself out here." Russ lifted his brows. "We've been keeping tabs on him when he leaves the tables."

He nodded, his pulse settling little. "Watch the money for the game."

Russ folded his arms, watching until Cavender disappeared around the corner. "Money's covered."

"I'll be back by the whistle." He held the old man's gaze, though he wouldn't let his guard down again.

Russ gave him a wink and turned.

Dalton continued on to the hotel, not surprised in the least by Cavender. He entered the hotel and made his way up the stairs, easing into Leona's room.

"Well, you didn't die after all?" He set his hat aside.

"So, you won more?" She smiled and met him with a quick kiss.

"Yep. You're feeling better then?" He placed her food on the small table.

"I'm better. Told myself no more spirits and slept even longer." She giggled and fanned her face. "I don't much remember the drink you gave me when those men roughed me up, but I sure remember this time."

He studied the bag across her shoulder. "You're working today?"

"Well, I ain't scheduled but with town so busy I figured Mary could use my help this afternoon while ya' play. And where's Gideon? He ain't next door." She sat on the small settee, rubbing her hand across the smooth velvet.

He nodded toward the soup. "I sent him to check on Ernest and Sable and told him to do his homework, but he was watching the games again. Did you eat anything?"

"A few bites of bread. What's that?" She rose and sat at the table to take a peek.

"Plain broth." He pushed the bowl toward her. "It'll make you feel better if you get down something a little hearty."

She wrinkled her nose. "I ain't so sure my belly has settled yet."

"If you can get this down, you'll be a new woman by tonight." He walked to her and touched her hair which hung loose.

"Tonight?" She blushed that satisfying pink he had learned to anticipate though she lifted a spoon and sipped the broth with a loud slurp as he sat across from her.

He frowned and unwrapped his sandwich from the brown paper. "Oh, I don't know, seems you were quite smitten with me last night."

"Lands Gambler...when you touch me it's all I can

do to try to be still and quiet." She lowered her voice. "You think I was too loud?"

He shrugged but grinned. "Nahhhh."

"Then tonight." She used the cloth napkin to wipe her mouth, sipping her soup this time.

"I should have poured you a sip not a glass. Won't be any wine tonight though. Can't chance you feeling poorly again." He took a bite of the beef and vegetables in thick bread.

"But you never took any of them there spirits." She lifted her brows in question. "You never do."

He shook his head and swallowed. "Not with the games or with you. Want my mind focused on what I'm doing. Like I explained about the bottle I carry, drinking and me just aren't a good mix."

"Who ya gonna play this time Gambler?" She ran a hand through her loose hair tucking it behind her ear. Damn, he wanted to do that for her. Sometimes he didn't understand what had pulled him to her, but when she looked at him with those deep amber eyes, it was as if she could read his very soul. Some fate he hadn't understood had drawn him to her.

"Just played Littlefoot. He's still in the games but he's down on chips. This time I've got Alice O'Hare and Edward Locke. And that Castle kid's still playin', he might be a bit of competition it seems." Dalton bit into his sandwich and then wiped his mouth, chewing.

"Well, you thought he wouldn't make a game at all." She sipped her soup again.

"Gambler, you're a starin' at me...again like you do." She sat her spoon aside as the train whistle blew the five-minute call.

"And I do like what I see. Later, madam. In the

meantime, don't work too hard, I want you back here to enjoy the few days in the hotel." He leaned down and lifted her chin and gave her a gentle kiss.

"I'll be a waitin', Gambler, right here in this big hotel fancy bed."

He winked and turned to head back to the poker championship.

Chapter Fifteen

Dalton pushed through the double doors, making his way to the assigned table opposite Alice O'Hare. The time had come, and she met his gaze with a suggestive grin. He gave her a quick nod and took his seat, leaning his cane against the wall behind him. He'd learned a long time ago about Alice. She was a black widow when it came down to poker. She played to win, flirting her way into the bank accounts of men she swindled along the way. The exact kind of woman he intended to avoid, since he'd had his knee blown out from under him.

She flashed her bright blue eyes at him, her painted lips curling into a smile. "Well, hello once more, Dalton Payne."

"Alice. Been meaning to speak to you, but these games get mighty busy." He removed his hat and settled his knee to comfort.

"I'll just bet you have." She adjusted the feathers across her ample bosom. "And here we are again, just like old times at the table."

"Just like old times." He agreed, not trusting her for a second. Oh, she wouldn't cheat but there was a lot about Alice not to be trusted.

"Seems I heard you'd retired from the crazy game we play." Her light brows lifted. "Though I suppose, keeping the wash woman couped up in the hotel has kept you plenty busy. Beneath your usual standard, isn't she?"

He folded his arms and leaned back in the chair. That she'd figured him was one thing, but he wouldn't tackle the subject to make things worse for Leona.

"Oh, well, you needn't worry over your little kept secret, Dalton, though I'd assume her quite a bit younger than the mature ladies you so often entertain." The smile on her face could have melted a bar of gold into the dirt.

"Castle's the name, present and ready." Leo Castle made his general grand entrance, dropping the two ladies he carried on each arm inside the door. Cheers from outside fanned across the room, the kid having assumed a following that adored him.

Dalton scrutinized the kid's pile of chips which all but matched what he and Alice held. Castle knew the game, but better than that he seemed to have a deep respect for it and that was if nothing else, refreshing as he gave a nod and sat.

The game had lost numbers of players leaving lesser tables full, each person with a heaping but varying amount of chips.

"Good afternoon, Miss Alice, aren't you looking as spectacular as ever?" Edward Locke removed his jacket and sat before his own lacking pile of chips. "Madam it's a pleasure and the same, of course, Mr. Payne. A large thanks for your hand in bringing the game to such a small a town as Wylder and with purpose."

The man's statements were not sincere, more of an insult to the town of Wylder. Locke had money, big money, though little skill at cards.

"What's the matter, Locke, no room at the Inn?"

He offered.

The man roared with mock laughter, drawing attention from the crowds outside. "Why there's no inn here for a man of my known status. Wouldn't you say Alice, the rooms here at the hotels in Wylder leave a bit to be desired by way of accommodations?"

"A bit shy of being spacious, though the boarding house serves well." Alice answered as the remaining player joined their table.

"Lady and gentlemen, you may deal the cards as assigned at your tables." Sonny stood on the bar speaking above the crowed and he rang the starting bell.

Dalton sized up the table and gave Russ Holt a nod. Things were beginning to wind down and not a soul at these games or outside the door could be trusted. A tough game with Alice, but maybe not so much the other men who's piles of chips held low. He touched the flask inside his coat gaining his focus. He placed his ante at the center of the table, but a ruckus and a boy's scream sounded from outside.

"Gideon!"

He glanced at his chips and back at the swinging doors. He had no idea what was going on, but he'd forfeit chips and the loss of a game if he got up. "I fold."

"Do tell?" Alice spat as he grabbed his cane and made his way outside the saloon, finding the bearings on Gideon's voice.

Across at the livery a man raised a strap to the boy.

"Hey!" Dalton cursed his leg, trying to get to the boy as the whip cracked again. "That's enough!" Dalton raised his cane and belted the man across the brow with a fist.

The man cursed swinging a fist that Dalton caught. "You son of a bitch!"

He shoved back and slammed the cane across the shoulder of the culprit, though he lost his own balance and bobbled.

The click of a gun sounded. Caleb Holt held a revolver to the man's head.

Dalton lowered his cane, trying to gain his stance.

"Hell of a way to die, Mister." Caleb didn't move as the sheriff made his way onto the scene; weapon poised.

"What in tarnation?" Sheriff Hanson yelled glancing at them all.

"I'd like to know myself." Dalton made one more lunge, but the sheriff held him back.

Gideon tried to get up but fell back against Leona.

"It's all right." She comforted the boy.

It dawned on Dalton as he glanced at his son. The man was the stepfather Gideon had feared. The Same one who left scars on the boys back, the same ones he'd wear the rest of his life.

"Who are you?" The sheriff asked.

"Names Reilly. Calvin Reilly." He nodded toward Gideon. "And that no good kid belonged to my wife. She died and he made off with all the money we had, the little thief."

Gideon jumped up, holding his brow. "You did it. You killed her. Made her sicker not paying a doctor to see her. And she believed you'd quit hitting her and quit drinking. You're a liar, that money was hers."

Gideon pulled free of Leona and ran, holding his blood-stained brow.

"No child deserves the marks you left on that boy,

regardless. He no longer belongs to you, he's my son and if I ever see you in the town again, I'll give you better than what he got. You won't take another breath if you ever show up in Wylder again." Dalton pointed at the man, pulling free of the sheriff.

Reilly lifted his hat from the ground, his brows narrowed. "Well, I see how it is, good riddance, sorry boy, never worth the two cents he got fed."

Dalton lunged for the man, but Hanson held him back. "Let him go, I'll see he don't come back."

"Move." Caleb pushed Reilly ahead. "You aren't welcome here."

Damn, Dalton could taste the blood he wanted, but as it was, he needed to see about Gideon, never mind the pile of chips he'd lost.

****

Darkness was closing in on evening as Doc Coyote stepped out of Gideon's room at the hotel and into Leona's room.

"I gave him something for the pain, if nothing else he'll rest," The doctor assured them both.

Dalton nodded, his pulse still racing at the idea of Gideon being hurt. This was his son now and no one was ever hurting him again. He'd become the Papa Bear overnight it seemed, and Reilly would meet his fate should he ever return.

"He took a good hit. I'll be back in the morning. Watch him for symptoms of a concussion… confusion or vomiting." Coyote grabbed his bag and coat. "I suspect he'll sleep and be as good as new by morning. I can take the stitches from his brow in a few days. It's not bad."

"Thanks Doc." Dalton shook the man's hand.

Coyote's wife Eliza Jane took a deep breath, and tugged her shawl around her tighter. "Well, that's certainly good news."

"Never seen a braver boy, never even moved while you stitched him right up." Leona folded her arms, walking closer to her friend.

"Leona, it's a lovely surprise that you are staying here in the hotel." Eliza Jane smiled and touched the sleeve of her dress. "And this is so lovely."

She admired her pink taffeta dress with a nod, hoping her friend hadn't figured out more than she should. "Dalton wanted me to have the chance to stay here, somewhere nice like this for a change."

"Well, you are so deserving of it." Eliza held her swollen belly.

The physician narrowed a gaze on him. "Be back come morning. You still in the games there Dalton?"

"Had enough chips to bail on the one game, but might be tough to catch back up." He shrugged. Hell, even if he lost all his three thousand dollars, it was nothing to him in the scheme of things.

Doc Coyote winked. "Well, hang in there, this whole town's waiting on you to win."

Eliza gave Leona a brief hug and took her husband's arm. "I'll see you come morning."

"All right then." Leona smiled and closed the door.

"Damn it." Dalton cursed and shoved his hands into the pockets of his trousers. He wanted to hit something, and hard. He's wanted to take Reilly right out.

"Ain't none your fault." Leona placed both her arms around him.

"He was afraid that Reilly would come find him. I

should've stopped it before it ever happened." He placed his arms around her pulling her closer.

"How could you know, Gambler. Leastwise the sheriff run him out of here." She rested her head to his chest.

"Best he goes back where he came from." He pushed back his anger as best he could.

"What of the game?" She lifted her head from his chest to look up at him.

He gritted his teeth and balled his fist. "I'll pick up where I left off. Might catch up with some luck, but it really matters little."

"It scared you, bad." She questioned as she took his hand. "My Pa used to say the hardest job you'll ever be is a father or a mother."

"It scared the hell out of me, just like when those men hurt you. What kind of man raises his fist to a child or a woman? That boy's back has been shredded more than once. Help me understand it. Should've killed him there on the spot." He grumbled and turned from her, smoothing a hand over his beard. He'd never had anger so fierce until Leona had been hurt and now Gideon.

She gave his hand a squeeze. "Then you'd be a hangin'. You and I both had kind fathers. Mine never laid a hand on me, my Ma either. But you did what you could, and we won't ever let that happen to him again."

He turned to look at her. "We?"

"Yeah. Me and you. Never let anyone hurt him again. Like a real family, looking out for each other." She smiled as if the whole world lay before her. Damn, that was what he loved about her, the freedom she found in adoring the simple things. All the things he'd wanted as well.

"I want that, you know. Me and you and the boy...something simple and happy. Lots of happy." His voice cracked at the idea of what he was about to do.

"Oh, Dalton we'll have that. I want it too." She hugged herself against his chest once more.

He let go of her and did his best to get down on his good knee. He tugged the small velvet pouch from his vest pocket and then looked back up at her as he took her hand.

Leona's mouth dropped open and she covered one hand over it, visibly shaking.

He pushed the gold band to her finger and then with tears streaking his own face whispered. "Don't want to wait one more second for you to become my beautiful wife, Leona. And this ring is my promise to you for forever."

For the first time ever, this loud mouthed tomboy of a woman he loved seemed at a loss for words. But then it came in the slightest of whispers.

"Yes, oh, yes, Gambler!"

Chapter Sixteen

Dalton stretched, glad to have yet another set of games behind him. He'd played a devil of a game with Poncho Gonzalez. The man never knew when to be quiet and chattered more when he had a good hand. A dead giveaway at what he was holding. But the quieter Gordon Conroy had said little, bluffing on the last hand. Dalton had called and that was that. Conroy held nothing and pushed over his pile of chips. He was done in this poker championship.

Dalton sucked in a deep breath. So, he'd made it to the final group of players as he suspected he would. Now things would get interesting to say the least.

The last five would play until all of their chips were gone. Ah, who was he kidding? Alice O'Hare would be at the table and that darn kid; Leo Castle had made it. He'd watched from the galley as the cocky young man had paid little attention to his cards and more to the faces, which had served him well. Poker wasn't always about the cards that were held.

And then there was Edward Locke, the man with all the money. It seemed he'd made it to the final five, which was a bit of a surprise given his ailing pile of chips in earlier play. Some had accused him of cheating, but Dalton didn't think so. He'd gone through the checks like all the rest and if he had cheated, Russ would have caught him. He was dangerous enough to make it interesting, though he wasn't sure the man could last.

And his last opponent was Walt Cavender, whom he'd managed to avoid until this upcoming play.

But for now, he had a break and stepped outside the saloon, headed toward the livery. The last of the sun was fading in the vast skies of Wylder and he needed to check on Sable and Ernest since Gideon was at the hotel resting.

He spotted Sable at the end of the corral, at the same time something hard had slammed across his back, knocking the breath from him. Another caught his shoulder. He grabbed the corral fencing trying to keep his stance at the same time an iron rod swung again. He dodged the impact, unable to see the face of the man who carried it or the other standing nearby.

He managed his balance and shoved into the men, fighting back with the brass grip of his cane. The bar hit his side and a fist caught his chin. He bobbled back at the same time the iron slammed into his bad knee.

He buckled, falling and grabbing for his leg. He rolled to his side as the barbs came across his back several more times. He tried to avoid them, but the pain curled him further. His breath didn't come with the shearing pain that rode up his leg to his back. The shock was so severe he could almost hear the gunshot that had first taken his knee as he fell into the dark abyss of pain that swallowed him whole.

****

Leona peered out the hotel window toward the saloon. It was no use. It was too dark to see much at all. Dalton should have finished with poker by now, leaving her to worry. He'd said he would check on the animals and then run buy to see Gideon before the games began again. She studied the ring on her finger and smiled, though she still watched out the window, concerned.

She peeked at Gideon, who'd slept most of the day, and who now slept across the settee in her room. Funny, the very boy who had tried to rob her of the widow's money was now her.... family of sorts. Like a son, maybe. The whole thing was strange that she should fall in love with a gambler man who had taken in a no name child and had now asked for her hand in marriage. Maybe it was as it should be, a misfit family, but in a way almost perfect. It was like she had somewhere to belong now, which was maybe what she'd been missing all along. Somehow the gambler had knocked down her walls, rebuilt her and let all the sunshine in, she would be happy forever and a day.

She turned to the knock at the door and rushed over to ease it open, expecting Dalton. Russ Holt stepped into the room, removing his hat.

"Dalton here?" The rancher asked, glancing around the room to where Gideon slept.

She shook her head, a panic rushing through her center. "Not yet but I was waitin' for him. Something's wrong ain't it?"

Russ hesitated but then gave a nod. "Not sure. Been keepin' an eye on him in between games since he's had bit of trouble with Cavender. The games been over, and no one's seen him."

A commotion filled the hotel hallway behind Mr. Holt.

"We found him, back of the livery." Caleb Holt stopped in the hallway speaking to Russ. "Someone's beat the hell right out of him, busted the leg."

A painful dread rushed through her chest. "I knew things weren't right."

Russ turned to follow his nephew. "Where is he?"

"Me and Daniel got him to the back room at the saloon, Docs with him. Don't look good at all." Caleb took off back down the hall in a trot. "Need to get back."

Russ turned to her. "Stay here, Leona."

"The hell you say." Leona let the swear word slip. She ran to Gideon, shaking the boy gently.

"Leona?" He rubbed his eyes, blinking awake.

"It's all right. I'm just gonna run out for a bit. You stay right here, and I'll be back. Don't you go nowhere, ya hear me?" Her heart raced inside her chest. He gave her a sleepy nod as she drew the blankets across him.

She grabbed her bag and followed Russ outside the hotel and into the streets of Wylder. Darkness had taken the town, but people mingled all over in twos or threes, mostly men. Who could have done this to Dalton? Cavender, the man he trusted least? And why hadn't anyone seen?

They rushed into the quietened saloon. Russ peered into the back room and turned to her, a hand on her shoulder. "Wait here, Leona."

She pushed past him. "I will do no such a thing." Dalton lay still with the doctor working over him. Eliza Jane was there as well, using a rag to clean his bloody face. Leona bent before the small cot and touched his hand, holding it in her own, not worried in the least about what the others thought.

Eliza offered a tender smile and placed the cloth into her hand. She dabbed at the dried blood but said little, letting the doctor work. Dalton's face and lip were puffy and purple bruises striped his chest and side.

Doctor Sullivan ripped open Dalton's pant leg at the knee. The look on the physician's face told the story. The knee was swollen twice its size and already purple with oozing blood from a gash in the knee.

"Dalton." She touched his hair, wanting to help him, but not knowing what she might do. Maybe if he heard her voice, he would relax with the doctor's care.

"Get me some ice in here and some light." Doc Sullivan's lips were pressed tight, his hands bloody as he assessed the damage.

Dalton growled and opened one eye trying to hold his leg. "How bad, Doc?"

Doc Sullivan ripped the pant leg further. "I'm afraid the kneecap is shattered. I'll get you something for the pain."

"No." Dalton's reply was weak but stern. "Gotta keep a clear head for the game."

Russ laid a hand to his shoulder. "Dalton you're done, son. Ain't no more game for you right now."

Sonny leaned inside the doorway. "Came all the way to this. He's sitting the final five."

"Whoever did this wanted him out of the game." Caleb leaned against the far wall; arms folded.

Dalton grimaced again. "Son of a …aaaahhhhhhh. Never got a good look at 'em."

"No doubts they knew you?" Russ upped the flame on a lantern and gave it to Eliza who held it for her husband.

Daniel rounded the corner and held near the door, Callum on his heels "No one at the livery's seen anything. None in town either. I let the sheriff know, but he's his hands full with two deputies on the bank."

"Just rest, no need to worry about the games now."
She tried to soothe Dalton, though if she could have
taken the pain she would have.

He grimaced again but tried to lean up. "Cavender.
Where is he?"

Russ bent closer, pushing him back to the cot. "He
knows we're watching him, but he made his way to the
Wylder Hotel when play stopped."

"Whose....watchin' the bank?" Dalton moaned, the
cot creaking under his weight. "Ahhhhh."

"You men step out. I can't suture this knee if he
won't settle." Doc Sullivan ordered. "This knee's a
mess, where's the ice?"

"Banks covered." Russ gave Dalton a nod and
grabbed a bucket of ice that was handed inside. He sat it
on the floor beside Coyote.

"You just rest now, you hear me? Ain't no game
worth your life." Leona smoothed a hand over his hair.
"Let the doc work. You're gonna be just fine."

Russ turned to Caleb. "Take the boys with you,
follow Cavender, see what he's up to. If he has men,
they'll show reporting to him at some point by my
guess. Watch out for yourselves, my guess is they
aren't playing fair."

Leona watched as the men trotted to do as Mr. Holt
told them.

She turned back to Dalton who yelped as Coyote
worked on his knee. "Shhh, just keep your eyes closed.
It's a gonna be all right, now."

The physician leaned closer, gaining Dalton's
attention. "Dalton, you got a couple of choices."

Dalton opened one eye. "Been through hell with
this leg, Doc, not gonna lose it now."

Coyote shook his head. "Nope, not talking about taking the leg. Best I can do right now is wrap it tight, keep the swelling down and hope it heals. Or I can take the kneecap and give you a better chance to heal. If I take the cap, I can order a brace to fit your leg, but you'll have to wear it all the time, even when you're healed. Either way, you'll be down for months."

He groaned in pain, unable to hold still. "Take the knee cap. Surgery then?"

The doctor nodded.

"Can the surgery wait a bit?" Dalton's voice was weak.

Leona caught herself wiping tears. Wasn't a surgery dangerous? How much more pain would he have to endure?

Coyote pulled splints and wraps from his bag. "Dalton, your game's over, best we don't delay much. I can wrap it for a while, let you rest. Keep ice to it to help with the pain and swelling."

Dalton looked from the physician to Russ and then Sonny. "Read the rules, there."

Russ frowned but took the blank contract from Sonny, scanning it. "All right."

Dalton blinked hard with his good eye. "Read the wording about if a player is incapacitated..."

Russ scanned down the paper. "If any player is present but becomes incapable of play due to illness or injury, the player may designate one person to take on the game of play in his/her stead. Should that person fail to meet the game, the original player will forfeit any winnings. A second player will not be name and fund forfeited to the tournament."

Dalton touched Leona's hand. "I'm designating

Leona Fabray to take my game of play."

"What? Dalton, I can't play for no poker championship." She shook her head, letting her mouth fall open her pulse racing hard.

Dalton squeezed her hand. "I can't name Russ to play given he signed on to manage the games. You hold your poker face, bluff when you've no hand. You beat me twice, girl, you can do this. I'll talk to you about each of the players. All you gotta do is know is when to hold the cards or fold. Hang on to as many chips as you can, lose little and watch the other players."

Her mind whirled at the idea. "I gotta watch Gideon and I can't play poker good as you. Besides, you let me win, teaching me and Gideon."

He nodded and of all things he tried for a smile. "You won on your own, I just suggested you watch how you played, no fidgeting. I know you can do this, and you do too."

"If you beat him even playing around, it's not a bad idea. I remember your Pa, he played the game well and he taught you, didn't he?" Russ chuckled, a sparkle in his eyes.

Leona nodded. "Pa taught me a lot of things and the first of that was not to gamble with someone else's money."

"Doc, wrap it up for now. You can take the kneecap later. Sonny, add Leona to the board when it's time." Dalton closed his eye with a grimace, his large body shaking in pain.

Coyote inhaled a deep breath and let it out, wiping his hands on a rag. "All right, but you walk on that leg at all, you could lose it."

He nodded though he kept his eyes closed. "You

wrap it tight then, gonna watch Leona play from that galley, like the rules say I can. You boys figure me out a chair I can manage."

"Dalton, I can't play, I don't know the half of what those already winners do about the game." She held both hands to his forearm begging. "I'm a gonna lose all your money."

He opened his good eye once more. "Get someone to sit with Gideon. You put on one of them fancy dresses and don't say a word when you walk back in here. And when that whistle blows, you take my seat. The chips will be there and all you have to remember is to play like you played with your Pa. Just a game of five card draw. One game at a time."

"But what if I lose all that money?" She questioned with a heavy shrug, squeezing his arm.

Dalton lifted a palm to her cheek and after a long moment offered another smile. "And what if you win?"

Chapter Seventeen

Leona sat with Dalton in the storeroom of the saloon. Earlier she'd found time to escape back to the hotel and put on one of her fancier dresses like he'd told her. A mint green smock style with small sequins that glittered with satin lace trim. The dress was so pretty she'd mentioned to Dalton, she could wear it when they married, but he'd smiled and let her know he'd be making the purchase of a real wedding dress for her. And now as she sat beside him, the thought of a wedding seemed far away. His leg would be months mending. He looked so helpless, his face swollen, bruised and battered, but at least he'd rested.

He winced, his knee raised on pillows and wrapped with cloths and ice to each side. "What time is it?"

"It's still an hour yet." She wasn't sure of what she was doing taking his place in a major poker championship. What did she know compared to the other players she would be up against anyway?

"You are the most beautiful woman I've seen. The men at the table won't even be able to focus, let that be to your advantage." He offered a smile that faded as fast as he'd held it.

"This ole' thing? Might be they mock me like when I went to church all dressed up." She shrugged and placed her hand on his.

He chuckled, but then frowned holding his thigh.

"Gideon?"

"He's fine. Sarah's a sittin' with him. Said she didn't mind." She touched his cheek. "Let the Doc give you something for the pain, please Gambler."

"Not yet. Listen. I know you're frightened. But you can do this...and I'll give you a few hints. Did they chalk up the names yet, official?" He nodded toward the door, his good on eye open.

"All of 'em even that Walt Cavender, that you think did this to you. How come they'll let him play if you know it?" She couldn't understand any of it.

"No proof. He didn't do this, but he was behind it, no doubt. Waiting for me to slip up...and damn it I did." His face contorted as he tried to adjust on the old cot.

"What do you think he'll do?" It was scary to think she would have to play the man. "Dalton, what if he tries to hurt you again?"

"He'll try for the win...Let's just say he'll play fair until he loses." He touched his cheek, where a bandage covered the stitches Doc Sullivan had placed to close the gash there.

"Don't touch, just rest. I'm scared Dalton, got you and Gideon all stitched up and hurt. Even if you teach me about each player, I've never done the likes of this here." She shuddered all at once, real fear moving through her.

He focused on her with one green eye. "You can do this. You'll throw 'em all for a loop they didn't expect. They'll never even think you can compete. So, when you're playin' watch Alice. She's sly but when she's bluffing, she will watch the one making the call. She never blinks if she hasn't a hand. Can't figure how I out play her every time. She'll bluff even with a winning hand just to stir things up, so she's hard to read."

Leona nodded as he winced in pain again. "I do wish you'd let the doc give you something so ya don't hurt, please, Dalton."

"Gotta keep my head." He went on, still clinging to her hand. "Edward Locke taps his fingers when he isn't sure what to do, which may mean no hand."

"All right and that young man, all dressed up what about him?" She'd been as surprised as anyone to see that Leo Castle had made it to the final table as young as he was.

"He pays attention. A good read on people and if you grit your teeth, he'll be on to you. But he bluffs well. Looks away if his hands not so good, talks more when he hasn't anything. Sit back and stare at him. Makes him nervous." He tried to adjust the pillow underneath his head.

She stood and positioned it for him, adding another. "There, that better?"

He nodded.

"Dalton, it's so much money. And you want me not to grit my teeth, my hands are shaking now, and I can't even focus on anything at all, 'cept wanting to stay beside you." She rubbed his arm. "I good mind to take on the Cavender myself for what he's done."

"Don't even think about it. I mean it. Beat him with the cards. You can play Leona, even if you don't win it's all right." He rested a hand to her thigh as she sat back to the chair beside him.

"But the money." She shook her head in protest having never even seen what three thousand dollars looked like.

"It's not about the money. I just need to finish the game and I can't do that without you." His voice dropped lower. "Leona this game is about more than money, it'll free me from what some think happened before. But you watch, cheating starts happening closer to a winner."

She nodded as he'd explained the details of long ago and she supposed it would be a good thing. "All right. But what about that Walt Cavender? How does he play?"

"He won't be expecting a woman in my seat, that's for sure. He has a tick, a bit of a stiff jaw when his hand's not good. And when it's good he says little. But he'll stare until you give up your own hand if you aren't careful, don't let him intimidate you. He likes to slow the game, idle it a bit. Leona, you have to play confident, like the money doesn't matter. Sit up straight. Hold their gazes. Don't flinch and take your time making each play. Don't be afraid to bluff. Play bold. Some hands will go fast, others much slower as it winds down. Don't guard your chips, take some losses with a smile."

"Dalton my pulse is racing so fast. What if I pass clean out right there in front of everyone?" She was not herself. Her heart raced, her palms were sweaty, and her mind ran in circles.

He studied her for a long moment. "They'll all know you are so much more than they ever thought, and I have a feeling you'll find some cheers when they call out your name along the way." He gave her hand a tight squeeze." Regardless how it goes, I get this leg mended up, we gotta lot of things to do together. Starting when I can walk, I'm taking you to see that mighty Pacific."

Leona bit her bottom lip to stop the tears. "The ocean, the real ocean, oh Gambler, I've wished so long for that."

"Then go play, Leona, like money matters little and show this town who you are." He held her gaze with a look that told her he believed in her.

She brushed back the tears, sniffled and kissed his puffy lips. "I was thinking, Gambler, it was you who saw me, who I really was all along. Like you opened some door that let the sun in so's I could see it, see a life we can share. Gonna do better than that. I'm gonna win for you."

"That's my girl!"

****

Leona stood in the back room of the saloon with Laurel. It had surprised her when her friend had walked inside, smiling in support. The first of play would begin in a short time and she hadn't been able to sit still, pacing with Laurel trying to calm her. She took in a deep breath, glancing across to the galley where Dalton insisted on sitting. It had been all Russ and Sonny could do to get him moved to a chair. He had his leg propped on stool and Doc Coyote had not been happy at the idea.

"Leona you're about to shake out of your skin." Laurel squeezed her hand, "You'll be fine, just play how your Pa taught you. You might do very well."

She nodded, straightening her dress. "Ain't never done much of anything like this."

"We'll all be cheering you. And you do look so lovely." Laurel touched her dress. "This is so beautiful on you."

"Ain't so comfortable, just scratches and itches, but Dalton picked it so maybe it'll bring me some luck." She gave a hesitant smile. "He shouldn't be a sittin' up there."

"Caleb said he wouldn't have it any other way." Laurel glanced at the galley and back to her.

"Doc says he can do surgery as soon as this is all over." She wanted to cringe at the idea of more pain for him. "Says he'll have a brace from now on, gotta order it from back East, but that Dalton can still walk fine if it all goes well. Oh, Laurel, I'm so afraid for him."

Laurel gave her hand another squeeze as the first whistle sounded. "He loves you enough to mend that leg so you can marry. Now you march right over there to your chair, and you give it your best and you wear that ring proud."

She took a deep breath and adjusted her dress once more, glancing at the band on her finger, the stone sparkling. Yes, that was what she would do, just like Laurel said. Give it her best, for Dalton. She studied him again. This time he gave her a wink with his good eye and looked away. That she supposed was to keep her from getting even more nervous.

"Leona, I have to go now, but I'll sit with Dalton. Caleb doesn't want me here, but I've insisted I am here to support you, of course." Her friend gave her a hug, slipping past her going to the galley.

Leona forced herself to glance around the entire saloon. Sonny was at the bar with chalk in his hand. The floor had been cleared of several tables to make room around the final table of play. Outside the streets were full of patrons wanting to watch, even more than the days before. She'd never seen anything like it and somehow as she talked to herself, she was ready. All right, girlie, as her Pa would say, deal the cards. She smiled in thinking of him. Wouldn't he be so proud now?

Cheers erupted as Alice O'Hare entered the saloon. She was clad as fancy as any saloon girl with feathers and a bright pink taffeta dress that matched her spit-shined boots and hat. She was stopped by Russ, who checked her hat and her purse for any items that might be used to help her cheat. With his satisfied nod, she moved to take her seat as Leo Castle trotted through the double doors. Men outside cheered him on as he tipped his hat. Why, he looked like a little boy dressed fancy for church, though Dalton had said to watch out for him.

She looked at Dalton who shook his head, not yet. She held her place.

A hush fell as Walt Cavender entered the saloon. It was Russ who met him at the door and began searching him for weapons or ways to cheat. Neither man said a word, leaving Leona to give a bit of a shiver. No, she forced herself to a deep breath and to relax.

Behind him, Edward Locke bowed to jests and cheers as he nodded to each of the ladies who made a grand show of escorting him inside. A man along with him took his coat, gloves and cane. They all disappeared, leaving him to his being searched by Caleb and then taking his seat.

"I reckon it's a now or never." She whispered to herself and with one more deep breath stepped up to be searched. She so wanted to look at Dalton but wasn't sure she could hold it together if she did. It was Russ who searched her small bag and gave her a nod to take her seat. The saloon fell silent as she made her way toward the table and took the seat between Leo Castle and Alice O'Hare. She straightened her skirt and folded her hands in her lap, keeping her head high and meeting the gaze of Walt Cavender. He never took his eyes from her, his mouth parting. So, Dalton had been right. She was quite a shock to them all.

"Ladies and Gentlemen, while I am sure no introductions are due at this point, the rules have stated a player who is ill or injured may appoint someone to play these games in their stead, once." Sonny held the chalk in one hand and the rules sheet in the other. "Dalton Payne was injured last night and is unable to play the remainder of these games. He has named Miss Leona Fabray to play in his stead, unless any of the forgoing players can find some reason his choice is not compatible with these games before us. All rights to winning or forfeiting the same."

The chatter outside the saloon doors on the streets seemed to echo and for a moment Leona thought she might vomit or pass out. She glimpsed at Leo Castle, who held out his hand in greeting.

"Nice to make your acquaintance, ma'am." He smiled and gave her hand a slight squeeze.

"Likewise." Leona tugged her hand back, heat rushing her cheeks. It was sure harder to be a well-dressed woman with manners than to be herself.

"I've no doubts what a man like Dalton Payne sees in you, a real beauty it takes to turn that man's head, been trying to get him into my bed for years." Alice sneered down her nose.

Leona fought not to let her mouth drop open. It was clear Alice meant that as no sincere compliment, so she said nothing, offering a forced smile.

"Oh, Darlin' no one takes me seriously. Go on and play the game, sweetheart, it's just a hundred thousand dollars up for grabs." Alice grinned from ear to ear, giving them all a wink.

"I'm well acquainted with the way of the game." Leona angled a glance at the woman until she responded.

"Indeed." Alice shuffled the feathers at her bosom.

"Welcome to the game, Miss Fabray." Edward Locke nodded, adjusting in his chair.

"Thank you, sir." Leona did the same, waiting on direction as Sonny continued. She was all but sure her heart might thump right out of her chest, but she made herself sit still.

"The games will begin now and continue until one player has the full pot of chips to their name. The rules have been read in full once more and you may begin." Sonny rang the bell.

Leo Castle picked up the deck, shuffled and lay it before Leona to cut. She took a deep breath, steadied her hand and did the act.

He picked the deck back up, gave a giant grin. "Five card draw, ladies and gentlemen. Ante up."

Leona waited her turn to lay her chips to the center of the table, following order and holding her face and her hands steady. She'd often looked on at men playing cards when she had gone into the saloon to pick up wash for the widow. It was very strange to be at the table now.

She left her cards on the table for a moment as she'd seen Dalton do. The others picked up or glanced at their own and the play began.

She lifted the edge of the cards, leaving them on the table. She'd a four, a jack, two eights and a two. Well, a pair. That was good right? Do not grit your teeth, she reminded herself. Sit up straight and play like with Pa.

"And here we go." Leo laid down his chips, scanning the faces at the table. "How's it gonna go, everyone paying to stay?"

Walt Cavender tossed his chips down, nothing showing across his face. No jaw tick so maybe he had a hand or maybe this was him settling in to play a bluff.

Leona did the same, discarding three cards and taking three more. A king and a ten, so she still had a pair. But Alice, tossed out a pile of chips to the center eyeing Walt Cavender who did the same. Mr. Locke eyed his cards, tapped his fingers and did the same. So, he had no hand. Maybe she had a shot here, but it was anyone's game.

Castle stalled, eyeing his cards for a time. "You're all playing a hard set here. Guess the money's calling to each of us." He gave a big grin and took his time counting out his chips.

Leona focused on Cavender and slid her chips to the middle with the next round of play. Dalton had told her to play bold and she had a pair, but doubted it beat the others. So, as it was, Alice was bluffing, and Mr. Lock had nothing. She figured Leo had the same, but Mr. Cavender hadn't moved. He had a hand, or he was holding hard to his poker face now to confuse them all.

When Leo tossed in his chips, Alice folded. "Well, boys and excuse me, Madam, I'm out."

Play continued on until it was time to show their cards. Well, she'd made it this first hand and it was still anyone's game. But Locke folded next, leaning back in his chair with a grin, his pile of chips dwindling further.

Cavender tossed in his chips. "Call."

Leo laid down three tens. "Read 'em and weep folks, three of a kind. Miss Fabray?"

Leona held her breath and turned over her pair. Two of a kind had not been enough. She shrugged without a sound.

Cheers filled the town with people yelling to let others know the youngest player in the games had won the first hand.

"Five minutes break, players may stand as needed," Sonny called out from behind the long bar.

She stood, as did Alice who studied her.

"What's it like then to have a roll in Dalton's bed?" Alice tossed feathers back from her shoulders, leaving Leona gritting her teeth.

"Well, if you must know…" Leona gave sly smile and leaned closer, "We've already broke one bed and we're a workin' on another I reckon. He's a roarin' appetite for it." She didn't have to wait long for Alice's response. The woman turned abruptly and took her seat with an "Umphh."

She tried to hide the grin that wanted to slip. Now she'd be the gossip of town, but she had little to care. She touched the ring on her finger and sat, adjusting her dress and focusing for the next hand.

****

"Well, I didn't win but…learned a bit." Leona sat beside Dalton on the next break from play. She'd had a bite to eat at Laurel's insistence and then took up the chair beside him in the galley.

"You did fine, just keep your focus one game at a

time." He offered a smile as he touched her hand, but it was clear he was in terrible pain.

"Dalton, you can't sit here for this whole thing, try to rest some." She pleaded, wanting to hug him were they not where they were. "Please, let them take you back to lay down for a time."

He shook his head, sweat rising on his brow. "I'm good for a bit more."

"Damn stubborn is what you are." Doctor Sullivan plopped in a chair beside him and changed out the cloths of ice against his leg with care. "I've tincture of opium, knock the pain right out for a bit. Give you some relief."

He tossed his head back. "Damn knee...pain ain't nothin' but that, I don't need to be out. Maybe in a bit."

Coyote got back up and went toward the bar once more to grab another bucket of ice.

She scanned around the saloon again. "It's 'bout unnerving to keep on readin' each player's face." She needed to be certain what each was thinking. "I'm afraid I don't much like being a gambler."

He studied her for a long moment. "You're already onto them. Now just play with that same drive you did with me that night after supper. Play big, Leona, play confident. When it's your deal, do me a favor, toss in deuces wild to the five-card draw. Cavender will know it's me talking, you'll bobble his nerves a bit. He knows I am well aware who did this."

Coyote returned with more cloths and the bucket of ice, touching Dalton's socked foot. "Your foot is warm. Can you wiggle the toes?"

Dalton wiggled his toes with little effort. "Sometimes, I've wished that doc back then had taken my leg. I think you are right on this kneecap, but it might be you have to take this leg, Doc."

The doctor looked at the knee again, "We'll see what happens when I get inside. I think the kneecap will do it and the brace will help, but I can't tell you it will ever get much better."

Leona's heart stopped. He couldn't hurt so bad he was willing to lose his leg, could he? She leaned closer. "Dalton, you promise me, if you will lay down and rest, I will spend every day taking good care of you to let it heal. But I will not play this game for you if you give up that easy. Now I didn't give up out there and I'm not a going to and you are not gonna give up here on this leg." She looked up as things quieted in the saloon with the lift of her voice to him.

Dalton gave her hand a squeeze. "Doc, I think I'll take a bit of something for pain once this next game is done."

Leona smiled. It would kill him to lose his leg and it would kill her to watch it happen. "And you know what I'm a gonna do? I'm gonna win that championship, you watch me, gonna outplay them all because they all think I'm nobody. Been hanging around saloons enough washing dirty drawers 'till I know how and when to play and how and when to fold those cards. They'll know who I am really good after these games are done."

He brought her hand to his lips kissing the back of it. "Never had a doubt in my mind."

Chapter Eighteen

Leona studied her hand as she took another card. This game was in her favor, though she had to keep her head and not let anyone at the table know it. She took a slow deep breath. She held three Jacks and if she were guessing, this would be her hand. Her chips were in.

Alice, beside her huffed, and shoved a pile of chips ahead. "Well, I'll see you, little lady and raise the pot."

Alice was bluffing if she knew anything about it. Mr. Locke laid his cards down, folding again.

Cavender took a look at Alice and then her and then Leo. He pushed his money to the center as well. Quiet again, he had a hand, but did he have three of a kind?

Leo leaned back with his arms folded and had not lifted his last card. He took a quick peek and pushed his chips to the center. "I'll see things."

She held her breath but then forced in air. Maybe she'd have a win. Three of a kind could do it.

Across the table, Cavender held her in his sights. "Well, Miss Fabray. Call."

She angled her look at him, laying out the three Jacks. "Three of a kind, Sir."

Cavender folded his cards with a glare. Leo followed and Alice made a spectacular show of laying her cards out one at a time. "Full house, for all to see, gents and madam."

Leona's heart sank. She'd been too confident and as she'd known, it was anyone's game.

"Fifteen-minute break folks." Sonny shouted from the board. He turned back to the chalking board and added their score of chips. She glanced at her ailing pile of chips. She'd won three hands, but it had been a while now since she'd raked some chips in.

She eased from her seat, wanting to sulk in disappointment as she sat beside Dalton once more. "Dalton, this ain't going so well, thought I had them with three jacks."

"I might have done the same. Leona it's all right, like I've told you. Look at me." He ducked his head to make her look at him.

"You're doing a good job playing the game, now focus on playing the people before you, not the cards. You said what you saw in each of them, now use it to your advantage." He grimaced. "I gotta lay down…can't…Doc can't do anymore."

Coyote stood and a whistle brought Russ and Caleb over.

"I'll get the boys to get you to the cot and I'll give you an injection to work faster." The doctor grabbed his bag.

"You finally give it up for a time?" Russ asked as he and Caleb adjusted the chairs.

"Maybe a game or two." Dalton nodded for her to follow.

Russ and Caleb got him back into the small cot in the storeroom of the saloon, but not before he'd yelped several times. Coyote wasted no time in jabbing a needed into his opposite thigh, though he didn't seem to even feel it.

"Leona." He whispered.

She bent beside the cot. "I'm here."

"Play the people, not the cards." He closed his eyes, and she ran the back of her fingers across his sweaty brow.

"I will, let that medication work, Dalton." She would do as he said, but she'd much rather stay with him.

He nodded and looked at her again. "I'll keep my leg I think, if I can just rest a bit without the pain.

"That's just what you do then, Gambler." She kissed his forehead.

The whistle sounded and she stood and straightened her skirt. Now she was more determined than ever. Cavender had done this to Dalton, or had it done and she wasn't about to let that man win. And Alice neither for that matter.

****

Dalton stirred from a restless slumber; the dreams vivid as he opened his eyes. He was still in the back of the saloon on a cot, his back now aching along with his knee. He'd have done better to have been moved to a real bed, but as it was, he wouldn't leave Leona or these games. His father's voice had found him as he slept.

Forgiveness comes in a lot of different ways, son, accept it humbly.

It seemed any time he heard his father's words it was the way of lessons he'd learned all his life, the wisdom that came from a father to a son.

"You need me to get the Doc?" Gideon was beside him, the boy's face still bruised and puffy around the small dressing.

"I'm all right. How'd you get in here anyway,

didn't Leona make you stay at the hotel?" He scolded as he pulled up a bit to adjust his knee.

Gideon let his gaze drop with a shrug. "Snuck through the small window in the other room. No one saw me though and I ain't causing no trouble."

Dalton let it go, not much he could do about it anyway. "The game still going?"

Gideon nodded. "It's taking a while from what I can hear but I's afraid to look out, or Mr. Holt might make me go."

Dalton peered toward the door, but closed his eyes. His damn knee didn't ache, it throbbed with every beat of his heart. The ice cloths fell away from his knee as he moved.

"Dalton…I can get the doc, he's right outside." Gideon eased the cloth back to his leg and started toward the door.

"No," Dalton fought to catch his breath, waving him off. "I'm good."

Gideon sat again, studying him for a long moment. "I've been good, stayed at the hotel, but I heard them say you got beat up. Do you think he did it? My other step Pa?"

"No, son, it was men Cavender sent, an old vendetta, like I told you. Reilly's not coming back, you won't have to worry of him again." He held his gaze until the boy nodded. He wasn't surprised he'd thought as much though, but he didn't want the boy to worry further. "I'm your Pa now, so no worries there ever again, all right."

The smile that came with Gideon's nod was well worth his choice in words.

Coyote walked through the door with his black bag

in his grip. "Thought I heard chattering back here."

Dalton eased up to his elbows.

"Thought you might like to know Leona's still hanging in the game, just won a second-hand pulling in a mile high pile of chips." The doctor grinned as he set his bag on the foot of the cot. "Gideon, thought you were assigned to rest a bit more."

"It gets a might lonesome in that big hotel and well, my Pa needs me." Gideon poked his chest out.

Dalton tried for a smile but let it fade with the pain. "He's no bother, Doc, but Leona...damn well knew she could do it."

The physician opened his bag. "Want something more for the pain?"

No, he didn't want his mind blurred, but the knee was gonna kill him yet. He nodded and Coyote drew up another syringe.

The doctor stuck the needle into the thigh of his good leg. Hell, it hurt, but not like his knee.

"Let it help you rest for a time more." The Doctor finished and went back to his bag as Leona trotted inside, cheers outside the saloon filtering in.

"Dalton, I did it, bluffed the whole table, even that Cavender and Alice. The whole town's going crazy. Hear 'em?" She was a flurry of skirts bouncing around in her excitement.

"Knew you could do it." He praised her and grabbed hold of her hand. "Keep it up, give them all you got."

"I gave him something for the pain, it's too much for him right now." Coyote glanced at her as he took up his bag.

"See, that's what you need, just a bit of time to

rest, let the time pass and I'll be right here after each game for a little while. We get that surgery for you, and you'll be better than ever. I just know it." She bent before him, touching his hair to smooth it out of his face. God, her touch was all he needed. He settled, the medicine working to ease his mind if not his leg.

He closed his eyes somewhere with the sound of her happy chattering filling the room and easing him to let go.

Chapter Nineteen

Leona folded, laying her cards face down. She tried not to let her disappointment show as she continued watching the others play. They had all played hard, but she had to admit Cavender made her a bit uneasy with his continued stares, even watching her when it wasn't her turn to act.

Leo Castle had laid down his own cards right before she did and now it was left to Cavender and Alice for this hand. Leona studied the woman and she never blinked. Bluffing then?

Alice moved her chips to the center. "I'll see you, Mr. Cavender."

He sat for a long moment, never moving and finally pushed his chips to the center, meeting hers.

The crowd outside cheered, all assuming these games would end soon, but it was as if the tension could be cut with a knife.

Alice moved more chips without any hesitation, another of her moves when she bluffed as Leona had discovered.

"Call." His voice echoed through the silent saloon.

Alice waited a long moment and began laying one card at a time on the table, never dropping her sights to view them. "Read 'em, Sir. Two kings."

"Easy money comes and goes with the wind it seems." He spoke in a calm manner, though his pile of chips had fallen lower.

The saloon erupted in cheers as Sonny called for the meal break of thirty-five minutes. She stood, glancing at her chips. By comparison she had almost as much as Alice and Leo, but Mr. Locke needed to win, or he'd be lost in these games soon.

Laurel walked up to her. "I've brought sandwiches, we can sit with Dalton if you like. You must be tired; you need to eat and have some tea. It will perk you up for the next of the games. Oh, Leona you have done so well."

"Thank you, Laurel and yes I might just need some perking up to keep this going." She followed her friend to where Dalton lay sleeping. Across the room on a pile of feed sacks, Gideon did the same, his mouth open as he snored. She only smiled, as she hadn't even known he was there.

"I suppose he needs the rest too." She sat on one chair and Laurel the other. "Dalton took something for the pain. Doc said he'd at least sleep through the next few games."

Laurel handed her a wrapped sandwich. "He needs to rest. Caleb said the bank is on guard still but no signs of the men who did this."

Leona glanced at Dalton and back to her friend. "He didn't want to sleep or take the pain medicine, but never seen a man hurt so."

"Seems he's had the knee pain for a long time, perhaps he's learned over the years to manage." Laurel unwrapped her sandwich and took a small bite.

"Suppose so." Leona did the same, surprised that the browned beef with cheese tasted so good. She must be starving as most often she preferred Chicken.

"Leona, slow down." Laurel added. "Eat slowly and we'll take a walk after we eat and get you outside for some air, clear your mind to start again."

She shrugged. "Guess I's just famished and didn't know it, come we can walk as we eat."

Laurel led the way outside the saloon where cheers from several met her.

"Don't give up, Leona." Chet Daniels tipped his hat as he passed by.

"Go, Miss Fabray, don't let them best you, bluff 'em again." Finn Wylder of all people gave her a nod from the steps of the mercantile. The two old men playing checkers on the porch tipped their hats. Old Mr. Wylder and one of the men she'd seen working at the livery.

"See?" Laurel touched her arm, "You're surprising them all, Leona. Everyone is so proud of you."

"Oh, there she is…" The Widow Lowery stood with her quilting women. "Miss Fabray we're rooting for you! Though it is the devil's game." The old women turned back to those behind her.

She gave a wave but followed Laurel on ahead. It was long after dark and she was tired, but so worked up sleep wouldn't have come anyway.

Laurel chuckled as they rounded the corner away from the dress shop. "Oh, gossip, gossip…. now, let's slow a bit and just walk, get our mind from the game and let you stretch your legs a bit."

Leona slowed her pace and took several deep breaths of fresh air. After the staleness of the saloon, she missed being at her pots in the fresh air. At least that was outside, though the smoke could be choking when the winds didn't cooperate, "they say no long breaks on the games now, just straight through until a winner. Guess it's good for me to get food and a breath of fresh air like ya' said."

"Leona we're all proud of you, but I am happy for you and Dalton and even Gideon." Laurel hugged her. "Imagine, you'll be married soon enough."

She nodded, her belly full of anxious butterflies. "Once Dalton has time to heal, we can marry after I suppose."

"Leona, you are so very brave with it all playing in the games. We should all be proud of the woman you are and the woman you're becoming." Laurel pulled a pouch from her pocket. "I made something for you."

She stopped and took the pouch. "For me?"

"Go ahead, open it." Laurel smiled, lifting her brows.

She was careful with the small ties and reached inside retrieving a small square bottle. "Oh, Laurel, it's so pretty, real perfume to match the other."

"I happen to know men cannot resist the smell of lilac, just a hint now and then." Laurel gave her a seductive smile as they carried on with the walk.

Leona opened the small glass and sniffed. "I guess perfume is next after all these dresses and skirts."

Laurel rested a hand on her belly. "Well, you are doing a grand job of things and you are beautiful and now they all know it. But I knew all along." Her friend beamed.

Leona studied her, and it was somehow time to tell of things. "Laurel, me and the Gambler…well, we…well, we kinda already…"

Laurel kept walking adding a shrug. "I've known that for a time, Leona."

"You did?" Leona let her mouth drop open, but then closed it again. Laurel was her friend, but she hadn't known she'd given anything much away about her and Dalton.

"It's not hard to tell when a woman's in love, and truly another woman knows." Laurel looped an arm through hers. "Your secret is safe with me. Leona, you love him and that is all that matters. Think of it, you and me. Neither of us here in Wylder thinking we'd find our loves and we have." Laurels British accent was such a comfort if anything.

"I thought maybe you'd think badly of me, but we are gonna get married, me and the Gambler." She explained though heat rose in her cheeks as she went on. "But you were right, I won't tell you the first time was easy, but it was nice a 'fore it was over. And it's good we found our loves."

Laurel smiled, she supposed as not to embarrass her further. "It's no one's to judge Leona, not at all. I am happy for you."

"Gambler said he wouldn't even mind children, think I'd make a good mama like you?" She glimpsed Laurel's rounded belly.

"Here." Laurel stopped and took her hand to the swell of her stomach.

"Oh, that's a strong baby in there." Leona's mouth stayed open as it happened again. "What's it feel like inside ya'?"

"Sort of the same." Laurel laughed as it happened again. "Like a kick as they say. The Doctor is thinking this baby is a big one already, though." Laurel leaned closer to her and whispered. "He mentioned there might be two."

"Twins?" Leona couldn't believe it, and jumped up and down.

"Well, we don't know for sure and please, I'm not going to tell Caleb but let him be surprised. Why, he'd just worry himself silly." Laurel turned them as the whistle blew the five-minute warning.

"Oh." She followed, gobbling more of her sandwich. "It's time again, my hands get all a sweatin' and my heart races inside my chest."

"Come on, we'll get you back and you can see Dalton for a second and then take your seat. I'll be watching again. You win this one. Show them all, Leona and I believe in you." Laurel hugged her as they continued on.

"Now I just have to believe in me too." Leona added as they arrived to the cheers outside the saloon once more.

****

Dalton woke to the quiet, uncertain where he was for a second until he spotted Gideon. He could thank the Opium for that and when he got to where he could take the pain, he wasn't going to take any more of it.

"Pa, she's holdin' her own in there, games about to end, she's up against that Leo Castle and the lady with all the feathers. It's quiet but they're sayin'; she's gonna take this game." Gideon used his hands to explain in all the excitement as animated as Dalton had ever seen him.

He tried to adjust his leg and lift himself to his elbows. "Sure enough?" He had to admit he was surprised Leona had hung right in there with the big names.

"No, you ain't supposed to move none. Doctor was

here a bit ago said to keep ya' still." The boy pushed him back with a gentle touch.

He leaned back, propping the pillow behind his head. "All right, tell me."

The lad did a quick peek into the saloon and turned back to him. "They're all just a starin' each other down, looks like."

While he'd never been anxious in his own games, this was altogether different. She was holding her own, and he was about to come out of his skin.

The kid was quiet for a time and then the roar of the crowd filtered through the saloon. He leaned up once more unable to stay still. "Tell me, boy!"

Gideon gave a shout jumping up and down. "She did it, Pa, faked 'em right out and had a pair of queens. She won again!"

"Son of…." He caught himself with the kid standing right there and didn't finish. "What's happening?"

"Can't see yet, the whole place just went crazy, can't even see her." Gideon jumped several times to see above people in the saloon.

It was a long while before Leona appeared in the door, holding a smile that told the tale. "I did it Gambler, you should've seen 'em all lose their whatsy. Alice couldn't even say a word and Leo just shook his head. That Mr. Locke dropped the game, said he's heading out since no way he can win now." She was hopping with excitement as she knelt beside the cot near him. "But Mr. Cavender, he just stared at me, rather frightening, but I looked right at him and smiled as I took his chips right over into my pile." She stood back up dancing around, "And my pile's as big as the saloon, even if I don't keep winning."

"I knew you had it in you." Dalton relished in her excitement, ignoring his leg as best he could.

"Oh, Dalton, this next games gonna tell it all. I ain't expecting I can win again but I sure made 'em all nervous as a fox in a hen house." Leona laughed as she hugged Gideon to her side. "Boys, we might keep a stayin' at that hotel a while longer."

He gave in and laughed as she and Gideon hooked elbows and jigged around in circles. And there they were, all he'd ever need in the world, given this damn leg didn't kill him.

"Got another break, wasn't sure we'd get one, but some are a sayin' this next game will decide it all." Leona turned back to him and clasped her hand to her purse.

"Let me talk to the both of you." Dalton was sure this next round of games would be rather intense and Leona at least needed to be ready for it.

"Gideon, you walk with Leona back to the hotel." He spoke to the boy and then looked at her. "Put on that satin red dress, pull your hair up, real fancy like. Get you and the kid something to eat and don't come back until that first whistle. I don't want you on the streets at all, it's not safe."

Leona folded her arms and angled an inquisitive glance at him. "All right, we'll be back as soon as we do that. Gideon will bring you something to eat."

He gave her the smile she needed to send her and the kid on their way and lay back once more. She was worthy of the win if she could get one more good hand or bluff well. Right now, the poker championship belonged to any one of them.

Russ showed at the door. "You ain't surprised?"

"Surprised as hell if it comes down to it." He eased up with some effort to lean against the wall behind him.

Russ nodded in agreement. "You hear all that out there, it's for her. About time she was noticed, seems she got you right smitten too just like thought."

"She's worked here a lot of years, no one paying her any bit of attention and look at her. The most beautiful woman in the room, upsetting the status in play. And soon enough she'll belong to me." He denied nothing at this point.

Russ took the chair beside him. "We've got trouble coming from Cavender if he doesn't take the win?"

"You've hidden that pot like I told you?" He asked, because while the bank was being guarded, the money wasn't there and that was a decoy to attract attention so no one would suspect otherwise. He'd asked Russ that much, to hide the money where even he had no idea.

Russ angled a glance at him, the man's face serious once more. "Locked tight. Caleb's only one besides me who knows where the money is."

Dalton nodded. It had been best he hadn't known either.

"Get yourself a bit of rest. I'll wake you for this last game, that revolver of yours loaded?" Russ lifted it from the holster checking and rolling the barrel.

"Always." Dalton answered and took it, setting it beside him on the cot.

"Keep it in your shirt, keep an eye on Leona. I'll watch the rest. Sonny knows nothing, neither do the boys, let's see how this goes. Doc's in on things. He'll come to cover you." Russ stopped at the door. "I'll have the boys move you back to the galley before things begin."

"I won't be no good to help Leona much, you watch out for her." He groaned with his leg once more.

Russ gave him a nod and disappeared out the door.

Hell, he couldn't rest now, but he closed his eyes, still leaning against the wall and listening to all the cheers and chatter from outside. He'd known there was something more to Leona when he'd first seen her in town. Or rather when she'd poured water across his boots. He chuckled to himself. What a luck of the draw he'd had then. And if they could put this poker championship behind them and his leg would heal, he'd take her to the Pacific Ocean. Hell, he'd take her to any ocean she wanted to see, and he'd spend a lifetime doing it.

Chapter Twenty

Dalton sat in the galley full of spectators, his leg propped up and a gaze on Cavender. His revolver was inside his vest for easy reach, his cane in his grip.

Sonny took the small ladder up and erased Edward Lock's name, leaving the four there, Leona Fabray, Alice O'Hare, Leo Castle and Walt Cavender.

He watched Cavender. *What are you up to you bastard, because I know it's something?*

The man turned back to the table as each player received their tray of chips. This game as it was, wouldn't take long and it was so loud outside the saloon, he could hear little. Leona nodded to the other players and took her seat, the last whistle blowing and the cheers erupting all around. And he was right, her dress and her hairstyle had caused heads to turn. Gods, she was the most beautiful women he'd ever laid eyes on and she was his. Or at least she would be.

"Folks, we're down to our last few games of this poker tournament, the pot of one hundred thousand dollars to the winner. We're gonna make a bit of history today for Wylder, let this town be known on the map of Wyoming as well as the whole United States of America." Sonny's voice rose an octave and the saloon filled with cheers and clapping, and those calling out to their favorite players. Outside the saloon the streets were filled to capacity, the noise almost deafening.

Leona glanced his way with a smile, but then turned back to the table before her. From where he sat, he could tell she was nervous, though as her chips were placed before her, she remained as calm as all. God let him get the knee well and he'd never spend time at anything but loving her.

"All right," Sonny stuck his pocket watch back into his vest. "Best of luck to each player and the game may begin. Play won't stop until a winner is named. All quiet!" The bartender rang the bell.

The deck of cards was placed in front of Leona, her turn to deal. She waited a long second, while each player placed their ante. She shuffled the cards, eyeing Cavender and then set the deck before Leo to cut.

She took it up again, "Five card draw…" And then adding a bit louder. "Deuces wild."

Cavender met his gaze with a hard glare. *You know you bastard.*

Two had always been his lucky number as wild cards went. Now he hoped that belonged to Leona in this game. But if nothing else, he needed Cavender's nerves on end and as it was his chips were as low as the other three players while Leona had a right high pile.

"Calm down girl, just play the game how you know." He spoke to himself, but she managed the deck and watched as the others eye their cards. She waited a moment and then pulled hers up from the edge of the table for a peek.

She waited for all to play, each putting in their chips down. And on her lay she discarded two cards and took two more.

All right, then, she had three to work with. Cavender held his cards as usual showing nothing readable on his stoic face. And beside him, Alice crossed her legs, glanced at her cards again and looked up with a smile pushing a large pile of her chips to the middle of the table. So, she had nothing. Bluffing.

"Folks, last game, gotta play a hard one, lot of money on the line." The kid chuckled and swapped one card with another; Leona dealt his way. So, chatter. That meant the kid might be bluffing them all.

Leona studied Alice, holding the deck and the woman discarded three cards and accepted three.

Cavender said nothing, but after a long moment of thought, sent two cards to Leona. She dealt him two more with a steady hand and full gaze.

"Good, girl hold him off." Dalton held his thigh, setting his cane aside and adjusting his knee. The Doc pulled up a chair as he struggled to hold still, shaking in pain. It might be that he should have stayed in the back, but Cavender couldn't be trusted. He had to protect Leona if things got interesting and he was sure that was coming. Some part of him should not have insisted that she even take his part. But he'd had no other options at the time. And darn what a show it had been with Leona at the table.

"Should've stayed in the back, Payne." The physician glanced at his knee and back to him.

Dalton caught his gaze with an added grin. "And miss all the fun?"

The Doc opened his coat, revealing a revolver. It was no secret Coyote was as good with guns as any of them. In fact, according to Russ Holt, one of the best.

He gave the man a nod, but took his gaze back to Leona.

The game progressed. Leo remained quiet, so it

would seem he had a little something. Alice had no hand, her lips tight and her hands steady. She'd bluff or fold.

"So here we go. I'll start with this." She slid her chips to the center, more than necessary upping the pot for them all. That was her notorious move at times to push games faster.

Cavender took his time again and lifted a look to each player. "I'll see you, Ms. O'Hare and raise you." He settled a stack of chips in the middle of the table.

Leo Castle whistled loud staring at the pile of chips. "Whoa, that's a heap of money there on the line, and this is as good as it gets in Wylder." The chattering meant the kid had nothing, but he bluffed adding his own stack of chips and turned his gaze to Leona.

She didn't glance her cards again, but pushed her pile of chips in place and waited.

Cavender laughed. "Well, Ms. Fabray, it seems you're a hard woman to figure. You've bluffed us all several times now. And Alice here always has her ways of leading the pack whether or not her cards show or not."

Alice cackled at his remark. "Well, it isn't a game for the faint of heart, Mr. Cavender."

"It's anyone's game now Mr. Cavender, is it not?" Leona responded with a confident tilt of her head.

Dalton could damn near swallow his tongue and the revolver in his shirt was a reminder.

"Well, dear," Alice turned her cards over. "I suppose it's been an entertaining game of play. I must fold." She stood, turning to the clapping of the crowd and curtsied. Damn, she was out. Something didn't add up or Alice had just lost to remover herself from

Cavender as she knew the man too.

"Seems it's a bit too steep for me. I'll see you fine folks at the next big game. Leo Castle folds." He laid his cards down on the table but kept his seat as the crowd cheered him.

That left Leona in a face-off with Walt Cavender. Dalton leaned up but the physician placed a hand to his shoulder. He didn't move further not breathing either.

Leona held Cavender's gaze for a long moment and eased her chips to the center. "All right; Mr. Cavender and I'll raise you as well."

Cavender's eyes narrowed. "Gutsy for a woman who knows little about poker."

Dalton eased both hands to his knee and settled his leg to the floor, uncertain he could even stand.

Coyote Sullivan didn't move, but eased a hand inside his coat. He handed Dalton his cane. Across the room, Russ watched Cavender as Caleb, Daniel and Callum held their posts nearby.

Cavender angled a smiling glare to her. "Well, now, Miss Fabray, it seems we're at the moment of truth."

Leona lifted her eyebrows. "Meet me, or fold your cards Mr. Cavender."

The hush inside the saloon was unnerving. Cavender began to laugh. He picked up his cards and took a long deep breath, pushing his chips to the center—all of them.

"Seems these games have come to an end." He placed his cards on the table. "Two king's little lady, how about we finish this game now?"

Leona didn't move right away, and the silence held. Dalton had to admit this was more unnerving than when he played the game for himself. He couldn't even swallow his own spit at this point.

Leona shrugged and studied the man and laid out her first two cards. "Two jacks…and..."

Russ stepped closer to Cavender from behind, hand on his weapon.

Dalton struggled to the edge of his seat and the physician stayed put, ready.

Leona put her third card on the table. "A four and…"

Cavender smiled, relief crossing his face. "And please don't hold us from the last two cards, madam."

"Mr. Cavender, it's been a real pleasure to play this game with you and these other fine players." She shrugged, holding the last two cards.

Dalton waited. Something in her voice had changed. She was about to win this whole damn game. Son of a….

"The pleasure's been all mine, Miss Fabray." Cavender studied the pile of chips and steadied his hands to pull them his direction.

"But I am sorry, sir, it seems that there pot belongs to me." She laid down her remaining two cards. "A seven, and, sorry to disappoint you in the games, but a two."

Cavender's gaze narrowed to her cards.

"Deuces wild, sir." Leona smiled and then laughed as the town went wild outside. The people in the galley cheered, clapped and shouted.

And then an explosion sounded, scattering those inside the saloon.

Dalton groaned with his leg, unable to do more than stand in place, his weapon in hand.

"Someone blew the bank." A shout came from outside as Leona gave a stifled scream, trying to pull free of Cavender who had grabbed her with all the commotion.

"Son of a bitch!" Dalton tried to move, but froze. Cavender held a knife to her neck and Leona quit the struggle.

Russ stepped closer, revolver on the man. "Let her go. Nothing good gonna come out of this and you know that."

The man chuckled, pulling Leona in front of him. "I beg your pardon, sir. You'll need to drop your weapon, all of you, or I will cut this woman."

Dalton cocked his revolver, the echo filling the saloon. Three more clicks followed as Caleb, Daniel and Callum followed suit.

Leona's frightened gaze met his. He held up a hand, holding her off, dropping his cane. He'd read her thoughts and she was about to fight.

"That explosion belong to you, Cavender? I reckon you don't know a thing about it, as you know nothing of Dalton Payne meeting up with havoc." Russ moved a step closer, his revolver aimed at the man's head.

Cavender narrowed his brows. "That's close enough. Mr. Payne's unfortunate injuries belong elsewhere, I assure you. But I am going to walk right out of here and no one is to leave this saloon, or this woman dies."

Dalton forced a step ahead as far as his leg would allow, holding his revolver poised. "Make one move Cavender. You know I don't miss or bluff."

The man laughed and faced him, Leona still in front of him.

"Dalton, you can't hit him before he hurts her." The doctor's whisper found him.

"Call, Cavender." Dalton managed a step, though Cavender didn't move.

"Call?" Leona shrieked and began slapping and punching until Cavender lost his grip of her. She turned and kicked Cavender right in the privates, doubling the man over. Russ grabbed him by the hair as Cavender held his crotch moaning. "Damn, that just smarts I'll bet." The old cowboy chuckled.

"You better think twice again, Mr. Cavender 'afore you put a knife to me again, that ain't very nice like." Leona kept on, pointing a finger at the man, the knife lost across the floor. "You ought to have known better than to think you could pull anything like this off in Wylder and with me you filthy goat sucker."

"Help me get to her Doc." Dalton leaned on the physician. If he didn't get to Leona to stop her, she might get hurt trying to take Cavender out herself.

"And another thing," Leona held her finger to the man's chest as Russ pulled him to his feet. "You the one who hurt Dalton's knee again, well, I'll have a say about that too…" She swung a fist that smacked the man right in the jaw.

Dalton managed to get to her and grabbed her as she yelped and held her fist.

"Let me at him, put a knife to me and hurt Dalton like you did." She scolded the man as others back up. "and what did ya go and do then, blow up the bank and that's my money you done blowed."

Dalton grabbed her into his arms. "Leona, enough, they got him." He hopped on his good leg and the Doc eased him into a chair.

Daniel and Callum tied Cavender, and the town went wild once more cheering Leona.

She turned back to him and bent still holding her fist. "And you, you're not supposed to be on that leg and if you think I am going to let you hurt that leg worse, you've another thing a comin'. Ouch." She rubbed her fist.

"That was a hell of a right hook. Leona, you won. Beautiful lady you took the pot." Dalton embraced her and took a look at her hand, though Coyote took her fist from him.

The doctor moved her fingers around. "You'll be sore, but nothings broken. We'll get it wrapped up. "

And then of all things she broke into tears and fell to her knees and further into his arms. Dalton held her. "Shhhhh, it's over, it's done, and you won, Leona."

She sniffled and looked up at him. "Gambler?"

"I got ya girl." He kissed her forehead.

"I's afraid, but I knew I wasn't gonna let him cut my throat." She explained though the full of her body shivered.

Dalton hugged her closer, ignoring his knee. "It's done. It's all over for him now."

"Sure, you thought it was gonna be, just like back then, huh?" Russ stopped before Cavender. "So, your little explosion didn't prove what you thought it might." He slammed Cavender back into his chair.

"This isn't over, I assure you all." Cavender spat, fighting his ties.

"Oh, Pipe down, sunshine." Russ patted his face with a heavy slap. "Sheriff's men will pick you up in a bit."

"Clear the saloon." Caleb shouted and the other

men went to it, urging people outside onto the streets of Cheyenne to continue the celebration.

Dalton eased Leona back from him. "What did you think, Cavender, we wouldn't be onto you, showing up to repeat the past?"

Cavender's lips drew tight. "This isn't over Payne. And twenty-five thousand is mine as runner up, I know nothing of the explosion."

"Oh, it's over." Dalton peered at the bar. "Read the rules Sonny."

"No weapons, no violence, no theft or attempted theft…should I go on?" The saloon owner chortled as he chalked Leona's name at the top of the board.

Cavender spoke again as Caleb got the man to his feet, handing him off to the sheriff and his men. "I'll get you, Payne, soon or later, it will happen."

"Walk." Earl Hanson pushed him ahead and outside, keeping a gun on him.

"Russ, bring Leona her winnings." Dalton gave her a light squeeze, his heart swelling with pride. "You're the most amazing woman I've ever known. Gods I love you."

Russ chuckled and made his way to the flooring in front of the long bar. He lifted up a board and pulled out the large canvas bag of game winnings.

Sonny put his hands on his hips. "Are you both kidding me, it's been there all the while?"

Russ walked over and handed Leana the bag. "You played a hard game, Leona, made a name for yourself and this town. Wylder's right proud."

"I never even seen this much money in one place." She smiled and showed Dalton the bag as Gideon ran to give her a hug. "Ernest is going to get the highest dollar oats I can buy!"

"You did it Leona!" Gideon danced around with her once again as they had before.

Dalton ignored his leg and forced himself up once more. "Folks, I'd like to introduce you all to the beautiful Leona Fabray, Poker champion of Wylder, and soon to become my wife."

Cheers and shouts filled the saloon and the streets of Wylder as he pulled her to him and placed his lips to hers for a brief kiss. "You did it, Leona and I never had a doubt."

She wept and waved to the folks hanging around outside the saloon swinging doors. She hugged him. "Deuces Wild, Gambler!"

"Deuces Wild, Leona. I love you." Dalton placed his lips to hers once more, tasting her happy tears until Gideon hugged them both. And in that moment, he held all he'd ever need in life.

Epilogue

Late Summer 1879

"Wait, wait, not yet." Dalton held his hands over Leona's eyes, moving her from the boardwalk and onto the sand. He leaned on his cane and bent. "Keep 'em closed. Pick up your foot."

"All right, but what are you a doing?" She used her own hands to cover her eyes and let him have her foot.

He tugged her boot off. "Now the other."

"Dalton, I know you are about to show me the ocean, but my hearts a beatin' so fast." She held out the opposite leg.

He removed the other boot, and then managed his own, adding them beside hers. The summer sun on the pacific coast was as bright as any morning he'd ever seen. A light wind fluffed her skirts and lifted wisps of her dark hair. "I think you'll be just fine, but keep your eyes closed, this is more for me than you."

They'd arrived at the coast, staying the night in San Francisco in one of the fancier hotels, a trip he'd been planning all during his recovery from knee surgery. The time had seemed long, and he hadn't been sure when he'd be able to make the trip, but his leg had mended well enough though he'd lost the kneecap and had to suffice to a brace at all times, even at night.

"Come on," He tucked his cane under an arm. He

grabbed her elbow as she was still covering her eyes with both hands. He led her down closer to the surf.

"Gambler, it's the sand and I hear the waves and..." Her mouth smiled and she smacked her lips. "Taste the salty air..."

He managed to get them to the surf, bubble-covered waves washing over their feet making her give a slight scream. Her laughter made his heart melt as he turned her to face the vast blue water. He stepped in behind her. "It's the ocean, Leona, the wind, the waves and the salt. As deep a blue as you'll ever see. Open."

She dropped her hands. "Oh, Dalton, I never thought I'd ever see it. Oh…. it's so big and a ship, I see a ship…. a real ship like in paintings and pictures in books."

She walked ahead and let the water splash against her legs, sand covering her feet and he followed until she took off running. She laughed and kicked the spray, never mind the full dress and skirts she wore. That was his girl, never afraid to enjoy each and every moment.

"Dalton, it's the ocean, the real salty blue mighty pacific…" She bent and splashed her hands through the surf and giggled. And she was beautiful, more so than the view she held, at least to him. And all he could do was adore her.

They'd married the week before, him insisting he wouldn't do so until he could walk on his own. With Gideon as his best man and Laurel standing with Leona, he'd watched her come to him with yellow flowers in her hair and the fanciest dress he could pay Laurel to make.

They'd left Gideon under charge of Russ Holt while they made the trip to San Francisco, the boy content to ride his horse helping all week.

"Dalton, it's so beautiful." She ran back to him and tossed her arms around him. "Thank you for this, wouldn't have wanted to see it the first time without you."

He held her hand. "Let's walk for a while."

"But your knee." She glanced down as his leg.

"Knee will be all right for a bit." He took her hand and walked in the surf.

"Oh, this is all I ever thought it might be, Gambler." She leaned into him. "But do you think Gideon's still mad and for that matter, Ernest and Sable?"

He shook his head. "Nahh, we can bring Gideon another time, this is our honeymoon, no kids or horses allowed." He kissed the top of her head. "Besides, Russ will keep the kid busy and by the time we get back, he can head right to school again."

"I suppose, but I've something to share with you." She looked up at him.

"Uh huh…" He angled a knowing glance at her.

"Well, I suppose we may end up scandalizing the entire town of Wylder with the news." She lifted her sights on him again. "As we've been married just a week."

He stopped her then. "All right, no bluffing."

She smiled. "Ain't bluffing, Gambler."

Dalton's heart raced, "You're sure?"

"That's right, a couple of months along." She smiled and now he understood the glow she'd been wearing for a time.

Dalton drew her to him and kissed her. "I knew it, something was different in how beautiful you were."

"I stopped taking the herbs a while back." She giggled and kicked at the water. "Good thing Doc Coyote told me it's just fine to keep doing what we do. I think we almost broke that hotel bed last night, Gambler."

"Ah, well, we'll see what we can do about that a little later on." He kissed her, tasting the sweetness of a love he'd never expected. He set them both down into the soft damp sand.

"Well, Gambler, we're all wet." She wrapped her arms around him, laughing and she sat beside him, the water soaking their clothing.

"That we are." He studied her then, and leaned into place his lips to hers gain as the water washed in closer, drenching them.

She gave a shrill scream. "That is the coldest water I ever did feel."

He peered out at the surf on the horizon where the ship was about to fade. "One day we'll take a ship to China or Africa."

"Not sure I'd like that." She took a deep breath and let it out. "Been a fightin' morning sickness a bit."

"No fun then?" He'd noticed she had a voracious appetite except for mornings.

She leaned into him. "Oh, Laurel tells me it'll pass in a few weeks."

He rested a hand on her belly. "Having my baby."

Leona's hands settled against his. "You think a boy or a girl?"

He laughed out loud. "We laying odds?"

"Well, maybe we should." She rubbed her flat belly. "How about five card draw it's a boy."

He shook his head side to side. "Nahhh, I'll play

239

deuces wild it's a girl who looks just like her mother."

She turned. "Oh, Gambler, I'll play however the baby comes, a boy or a girl. Happy?"

He turned her back to face him. "You, Leona are a whole life I never thought I'd have, never thought I could walk away from the cards, settle and want that every day, but I do…with you."

"Gambler?".

"Huh?"

"I never thought I was beautiful until you." She hugged him.

He kissed her. "Damn near take my breath just looking at you and I'm gonna make sure you know how beautiful you are every day I draw breath."

"You can always make me blush." She whispered as she leaned in to kiss him. "Can we come here again?"

"We can come here all week and other times when you want to make the trip." He'd held her tighter. "All I want is to see your smile every day, Leona."

"Gambler?" She asked as she stood and helped him to his feet.

"Huh?"

"What about we go and try to break that bed this time?" She pressed her lips tight but then giggled.

"You are a dangerous woman." He helped her up and turned them back the way they had come.

"Sent a right hook once ya know." She showed him her fist.

"I'd rather just break that bed you are talking about." He stopped and pulled her to him, taking her lips and holding her against him as if she were his very world, after all she was.

****

Summer 1881

Dalton woke before dawn as usual. He glanced at Leona, who slept with tiny Gracie at her breast. He studied the picture of them together, his daughter's hair the same dark color as her mother's. He ran a palm across the infant's small head and smiled. He rose from the bed as not to disturb Leona. He stepped into his trousers, tied the brace to his bad knee and limped across the room. His leg was the reason for the lack of sleeping as it always would be.

He and Gideon has plowed a field for wheat, something new to them both, and while he appreciated the hard work next to the kid, his leg was sore. His movement stirred Gabriel from his sleep. The toddler stood in his crib across the room with a whimper. "Papa."

"Hey boy. Come here." Dalton lifted his son, wrapping the small blanket around him and escaped the room to allow Leona her rest.

Gabriel curled into him sleepily. He made his way outside to the porch and sat in the rocker. He smiled, sitting on the porch early mornings in the dark breathing in the crisp air, one of his favorite things. Across from the corral in the open fields Sable and Ernest grazed on the tall grass with Lucky, the quarter horse he'd promised Gideon for staying in school.

He hugged Gabriel's small body to him and sucked in the last of the night air. Content. A word he'd never bothered to hang on to in his past and now the pleasure of each day on the homestead somehow a reward for all the past he might not have done so right.

He had all he'd ever need in glancing around the homestead. His father's land and somehow his Pa's voice still with him. A beautiful feisty woman he couldn't stand to be two feet away from and children. What more did any man need?

Oh, there were crazy days, he and Gideon had to chase Ernest ten miles when a fox had entered the corral. The mule had run the beast off into the woods and kept going. Leona had taken on more sewing at home from the dress shop and had been content to do so from home.

Gabriel moaned in his sleep. The boy would be two years old in a few weeks and he was already a spitfire talker like his mother. No doubt little Gracie would be much the same. She already had her own little spirited temperament he'd grown to adore.

He hadn't thought much about children until Leona. But, they made him feel young. Gideon was doing well in school and did a heap of work in helping him on the homestead, the hard work bringing them closer as time had passed. There were times he couldn't remember what life was like without his brood. Life was precious. He lifted his young son's small, soft hand and kissed the back of it.

And his children were blessed. They had Leona for a mother, and it had been his joy to watch her become a good one. She'd delivered both her children as if she was born to it and was already talking about another.

He pulled the blanket snug over his son. Even with having money she still lived the day to day with simplicity. She'd take the children with her to town, insisting it was fine and showing them off. She still spent a lot of time at the Holt ranch with her friends. He fathomed she enjoyed all the attention in town that still rang out from time to time about her poker championship. Well, she deserved that didn't she?

Inside the baby began to fuss. Leona's soft voice rang out in a soft lullaby, more comfort to him than to the baby he thought. She was such a good and patient mother, and her happiness would warm him for a lifetime, now and always.

He closed his eyes and rocked his son to the slow pace of her continued humming. And his reward? A lifetime of holding the beautiful Leona in his arms.

A word about the author...

Kim Turner writes western historical romance, and discovered her passion for writing at the age of eight.

Kim graduated with a Bachelor's of Science in Nursing and holds a Master's Degree in Adult Education. Working as a registered nurse educator for over thirty years, she enjoys studying the medical treatments of the old west as well as keeping up with the latest western movies and television series.

While she loves reading anything from highlanders to pirates, she claims to have an unquenchable thirst for the American Cowboy when choosing her reads.

Kim lives south of Atlanta with her husband and calls her greatest accomplishment the birth of one daughter and the adoption of another from China, neither of which came easy.

Kim's Motto: It's All About A Cowboy and the Woman He Loves.

kimturnerwrites.com